*Three Homes for the Heart*

# Book I

# The Paper House

*By*

**Dorothy Minchin-Comm**

Order this book online at www.trafford.com
or email orders@trafford.com

Most Trafford titles are also available at major online book retailers.

Printed in the United States of America.

ISBN: 978-1-4669-0812-3 (sc)
ISBN: 978-1-4669-0813-0 (e)

Trafford rev. 02/10/2012

 www.trafford.com

North America & International
toll-free: 1 888 232 4444 (USA & Canada)
phone: 250 383 6864 ♦ fax: 812 355 4082

# Dedication

To Dad and Mum,

Gerald and Leona Belle Minchin,

the loving architects of my childhood,


*and*


To all Other Parents,

whose ideals and dedication have also built strong families,

homes from which their children may walk out into life

in faith and confidence.


*"If I could have chosen my parents and designed my own childhood,*
*I could not have devised anything better than what I actually had."*
*Gary Marais, MD (2010)*

# Table of Contents

# Introduction

Remain within the family or become public? In my case, publication certainly was not my primary motivation. I simply wanted to savor and understand the joys, the puzzlements, and the wonder that have been mine.

Moreover, I must confess to writing from an unabashedly prejudiced viewpoint. My family is the best, and I will debate the point with whoever wishes to take the matter up with me. *The Paper House* demonstrates the powerful ties of heredity. It particularly celebrates cousins! They are those people who are so strangely like us and yet different. Sometimes even exotic! As one of the most supportive of all relationships, "cousining" has made my family wider and warmer and has enriched our sense of clan.

Against this hopelessly biased viewpoint, then, what right do I have to unload more words—personal ones at that—onto a world already glutted with printed matter? I think of at least three reasons.

First, psychologists tell us that our first twelve years are, in many ways, the most sensitive time of our lives. Unencumbered by adult pomposity and evasion, children live with one another, cope with parents, and confront the universe with a simple honesty. That stance and that freedom, I believe, is something worth recalling.

Second, in our utterly fragmented world, we all want to know where and how we fit in. We're pathologically eager to "belong." Whether we like it or not, our family, our bloodline, can never be taken away from us. We need to recognize those ingredients—cultural, physical, and spiritual—that went into the making of us.

Finally, domestic abuse too often stands center-stage in our media.

Perhaps a little effort spent unrolling some of the old blueprints and celebrating a few of those ideals that make up happy families will be time well spent.

Thus, opening the door of my *Paper House* should give you a certain pleasant "shock of recognition." Walk with me companionably through the rooms. Childhood was once a very real house, full of good food and good fun, laughter and tears, big people and little people.

Then, inevitably, that door closed.

My home that has now been remodeled in paper, however, is no less real. Come in! The welcome mat is out.

**Dorothy Minchin-Comm, PhD**
Professor of English *(Retired)*
La Sierra University
Riverside, California
2012

# Acknowledgements

***Cover Design:*** Born in County Surrey, England, the internationally known sculptor, Alan Collins, designed the front cover. (Kara Lewis later extended it to the back cover). He and Dorothy Minchin-Comm were, for some years, colleagues on the faculty of La Sierra University. Together they produced three multimedia programs. The first, "Ages of Man," was particularly well-traveled. Apart from his many art works in London and elsewhere in the British Isles, Collins' powerful sculpted figures have become icons on several university campuses, including Loma Linda

**Alan Collins**

and La Sierra (California), Andrews (Michigan), Oakwood (Alabama), Walla Walla (Washington), and Canadian University College. One of his coats-of-arms stands at the entrance to Parliament House in Kampala, Uganda.

At twenty-four years old, Kara Lewis had graduated with a master's degree in Interdisciplinary Studies from the Southern Oregon University (2009). While developing her skills in photography, painting, and drawing, she works in her family's art business, Lewis Enterprises (http://lewisenterprises.blogspot.com). She designed the covers for the next two books in the series. For this book, she provided the artwork for the back cover.

**Kara Lewis**

Fern Sandness-Penstock

***Chapter Illustration:*** Fern Sandness-Penstock has been a lifelong friend of Dorothy Minchin-Comm, ever since they first met as juniors in high school in Canada. She has traveled worldwide with her husband, Floyd, a teacher and school administrator. Because of her multiple artistic interests, Fern's sketch book has never been far from her side. She was well qualified to read the three manuscripts for *Three Homes for the Heart* and distill out of each chapter one image that captured the essence of that stage of the story.

Richard Weismeyer

***Layout and Design:*** Richard Weismeyer, the long time head of the Department of University Relations at Loma Linda University, began work on *Three Homes for the Heart*. It was the last of several projects on which this enthusiastic, capable man and the author collaborated. After he died in January, 2011, his colleague, Larry Kidder, completed the unfinished task—with equal skill and flair. Larry has worked in the Office of University Relations at Loma Linda University for close to 20 years.

Larry Kidder

# *By the same author ...*

## BOOKS

1. Yesterday's Tears (1968)
2. To Persia with Love (1980)
3. A Modern Mosaic: The Story of Arts (1981)
4. His Compassions Fail Not (1982)
5. Encore (1988)
6. Gates of Promise (1989)
7. A Desire Completed (1991)
8. Curtain Call (1999)
9. Glimpses of God (1999)
10. The Winter of Their Discontent (2004)
11. Health to the People (2006, with P. William Dysinger)
12. The Book of Minchin (2006)
13. The Celt and the Christ (2008)
14. An Ordered Life (2011)
15. The Paper House (1990, 2012)
16. The Bamboo House (2012)
17. The Gazebo (2012)
18. The Trials of Patience Dunn (2012, in progress)
19. A Song for David (2012, in progress)

20-24. My World: A Personal View [Travel journals, 4 volumes]
    I. The Far East Revisited: A Term of Service (1970-1974)
    II. Return to Service in the Far East (1974-1978)
    III. Home Base: Southern California (1978-1988)
    IV. Retirement and Other Adventures (1989-2010)

## ACADEMIC RESEARCH AND BOOK-LENGTH SYLLABI

1. The Changing Concepts of the West Indian Plantocracy in English Poetry and Drama, 1740-1850. [Doctoral dissertation, 1971]
2. The Bible and the Arts (1974, 2001)

3-4. Studies in the Humanities (1977, 1979). [2 volumes]
5. Discovering Ourselves Through the Arts (1981)
6. Christianity in India. [Monograph, 1992, 1995, 1996]
7. Archdeacon Thomas Parnell. [Monograph, 1992, 1995, 1996]

## OTHER

Miscellaneous articles, news stories, biographical sketches, multi-media scripts, and editing assignments.

# Part I

# The American Beginnings

# American Beginnings

My American grandparents came of pioneer stock, both of their families having followed the western trails from Pennsylvania and New England.

Grandfather Bert Rhoads always revered his mother, Fietta Himes. Her first husband, Henry Rhoads, had fought and died in the Civil War. When his brother Harrison returned from the Tennessee battles, he married the widow and fathered four children. The family situation was not, however, a happy one. Young Bert left home early, took up a homestead in Iowa, and married Mary Rowland of Sutherland.

With his sturdy Pennsylvania-Dutch and Swiss background, Grandpa lived a life of incredible endurance. For more than fifty years he taught elementary school. He thought nothing of walking to school, a ten-mile round trip, the South Dakota winter notwithstanding. His pupils adored him. worshipped him, in fact. He could often be seen trudging through a schoolyard with a child hanging on each finger. Yet probably no man ever lived on God's green earth who had a clearer vision of right and wrong, of justice and corruption, than did Grandpa Rhoads. For him the world was black and white, unrelieved by any shade of gray. No question. No debate.

Grandma, on the other hand, came of gentle English parentage. Her sensitive nature and artistic gifts somehow mellowed the harsh frontier setting that was her home. She reared their family of five, often alone. For years Grandpa traveled through Iowa and the Dakotas as a school inspector. He walked literally hundreds of miles, carrying his rock-heavy leather suitcase. When he taught school, he'd leave at 4 a.m. and not return until late suppertime. Grandma brought some distinguished relationships into the family: her mother was Carrie Huxley, of the family of famous Huxleys (Thomas, Aldous and Sir Julian). She was also related to President Woodrow Wilson. (Her

**Bert and Mary Rhoads of the Dakotas and Iowa, U.S.A. (Parents of Leona Belle Rhoads). Front, from left: Bert Rhoads, Leona Belle, Mildred, Mary Rowland-Rhoads. Back, from left: James Rhoads, Norma Rhoads-Youngberg, Ruth Rhoads-Bresee (June, 1917).**

brother Wilson Rowland looked enough like the President to discourage any refutation of kinship.) And she had two distant New England grandfathers who fought as colonels in the American Revolution. Then, beyond all of that, the Rowlands traced their lineage all the way back through England, Wales and France to Roland, the nephew of King Charlemagne, the epic hero who died in 778 A.D.

Yet none of these curious connections made any difference in the simple little mid-western Rhoads home that I knew. I learned about these things much later in life.

Grandpa and Grandma toiled to give their three younger children what they never could dream of having themselves, a college education. The elder daughters, Norma and Ruth, married young, right out of high school. The former went as a Christian missionary to the Far East, and the latter died in the influenza epidemic in 1918 in the first year of her marriage. The other three, James, Belle and Mildred, however, all went to Union College in Lincoln, Nebraska.

There the tall, beautiful Leona Belle attracted the attention of one of the

John and Martha Ellen (Hitchcock) Minchin of Western Australia (parents of Gerald Minchin). Front, from left: Gerald Minchin, Martha Ellen Hitchcock-Minchin, John Minchin, E. Lennard Minchin. Back, from left: Florence Minchin-Laird (holding Baby Ken), Jack Laird, Victor Minchin, Ruby Minchin, Harold Minchin (about 1907).

most exotic students on campus, Gerald Hopetoun Minchin, from Western Australia. He surprised many of the corn-country young people with his ability to read and write English. (Ironically, he soon became editor of the campus newspaper, *The Clocktower*). His courage in riding streetcars amazed them, and he also bore other unexpected marks of civilization. Rather than tell his American classmates what Australia was really like, however, he just enjoyed the comedy and let them go on in their ignorance.

After the premature deaths of both of his parents, Gerald had decided on studying in America. He sold his piano to pay for his trans-Pacific ticket. He had some detours on the way, however, and the money ran short. His ship docked in Honolulu for a few days, but he stayed on for three years. He spent the interim teaching at Hawaiian Mission Academy, climbing volcanoes and learning Hawaiian guitar. Then he worked a couple of summers in widely assorted jobs. First as a lumberjack in southern Oregon (1924) and then as a hospital orderly in Los Angeles County Hospital, California (1926).

Finally, he continued his eastern trek to Emmanuel Missionary College in Michigan which was his ultimate goal. Stopping briefly in Lincoln, however, he met W.W. Prescott, an administrator who had once worked in Australia.

*Left:* Gerald Hopetoun Minchin, born in Cottesloe, Western Australia (1901), became one of the most exotic students on campus when he arrived at Union College, Nebraska, in 1926. *Right:* Leona Belle Rhoads, born in Elk Point, South Dakota (1907), soon fell in love with the "alien" from Australia.

Taking a special interest in the young transient, Prescott inquired, "Why go to Michigan? What's wrong with staying here for school?"

Gerald could think of no real reason, so he stayed. When he met Leona Belle Rhoads, Professor Prescott's secretary, he couldn't think of going anywhere else to look for anything.

On being introduced, however, Gerald blurted out, "Oh, we have a cow at home by that name … Belle." The words popped out involuntarily. He quickly surmounted his initial blunder, however, and went on to overcome even more serious barriers.

One was acceptance by the Rhoads family. No problem with the younger sister Mildred, but Bert and Mary Rhoads, along with the rest of their family and friends, had a rather narrow experience. They knew of little that came from Australia except kangaroos. More difficult yet was Grandpa's basic assumption that probably there weren't any men in the world really good enough to marry any of his daughters anyway.

Still the courtship proceeded unchecked. Both Gerald and Belle worked in the college kitchen, and their classmates sometimes accused them of holding hands under the dishwater.

In the spring, Gerald proposed to Belle one night after a concert. Because of the pressure of severe chaperonage at the college, he had little time or opportunity to make his case. He snatched a kiss and rushed it under the staircase in the old Administration Building. The couple married on August 22, 1928, in Topeka, Kansas.

Thus a complete cast of characters came together. The stage was set for the arrival of one person. ME!

*Above:* Marriage of Gerald Minchin and Leona Rhoads on August 22, 1928, in Topeka, Kansas. *Top right:* Dorothy Belle Minchin, born prematurely on October 17, 1929. She made a traumatic appearance, very nearly causing the death of both her mother and herself. *Right:* The new Gerald Minchin family at a summertime picnic in Topeka, Kansas (July 1930).

Gerald proudly claimed his firstborn daughter, Dorothy. The car, however, served as a mere backdrop (it would be another seven years before he would possess an automobile of his own).

# CHAPTER 1

# Up to Date in Kansas City

The goal took more than forty years to accomplish, but it was worth it. A few years ago I finally made my private pilgrimage to Kansas City, to where everything began for me.

I can't remember how many times I've crossed and re-crossed the United States. It must be more than a dozen, at the very least. Still, I could never interest my parents, my husband or my children in taking the necessary detour to return me to the old schoolyard at 3023 South Monroe Street, in Kansas City, Missouri. We were always too far north, too far south, and forever in a hurry.

Dad and Mum's lack of interest I can understand. To them Kansas City represented three of the hardest years of their lives. There they tasted the dregs

 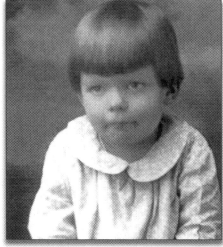

*Left:* **Skilled seamstress that she was, Grandma Rhoads made this coat and matching bonnet for Dorothy (age 2 ½). Already the child's lifelong aversion to hats is evident.** *Right:* **The results were far-reaching. Even** *without* **the hated bonnet Dorothy remained a little depressed.**

of the Great Depression, teaching together in an eight-grade elementary school (full time) for the sum of $75.00 a month. No wonder they both put up a mental block, a buffer zone between themselves and the Kansas City years.

For me, on the other hand, my journey backward in time opened the door to my beautiful Paper House. These things, of course, are simply a matter of viewpoint. I felt a warm, direct kinship with the old hurdy-gurdy merry-go-round in the playground when I sat down amid its rusty irons and splintered boards. I looked up at the old stucco schoolhouse, noting especially the windows and the steps to our little apartment at the back of the two classrooms. Once again, I walked over the heaved-up sidewalk (literally dated 1898) and realized that no maintenance had been done since I'd been there the last time.

An old black man sitting on the porch next door watched me making my quest into the past. He seemed as pleased as I in my recognition of my old home. "But they done tore out all the insides, Ma'am," he said. "Now it's our church."

The little store on the corner of the street has now metamorphosed into

**Gerald Minchin in front of the Wichita Intermediate School (1931), caught in the toils of the Great Depression. As principal, he sat in the middle of his little flock, knowing full well that in the summer months his paycheck would disappear.**

an auto-repair shop. Once in a long while I used to have a few pennies to spend for a treat at the store. It was the first public place I ever went to alone! Permission granted only because I didn't have to cross the street in getting there.

When Gerald Minchin graduated with his BA in English at Union College in Lincoln, Nebraska (1933), he had set something of a precedent for the times. Few college students married before graduation. During his junior year, he served as Editor-in-Chief of *The Clock Tower*, campus paper (1931-1932). In his editorials, he fearlessly addressed subjects ranging from the pitfalls of industrialism to the rudeness of the student body at a formal music concert.

After an hour I'd completed my vigil. Materially speaking, childhood and all that the Kansas City home meant to me is long since gone. Yet my visit gave me a very perfect little vignette, a blueprint for the Paper House I always wanted to build. As my son Larry and I drove out of the city, heading west through the Kansas cornfields, I finally felt complete. I knew I wouldn't have to return to Kansas City again. Also, I could understand how the sweaty industry and faceless dullness of that part of the city, especially the river flats, must have vexed my father's intellectual, beauty-loving soul.

Back in 1928 Dad had interrupted his academic career, encumbering himself first with a wife and then a child. Afterwards he spent two dust-bowl years of teaching in Liberal and then in Topeka, Kansas. Then he returned to Union College.

My parents rented a small downstairs apartment near the campus. Mum's younger sister, Mildred, lived with us, and became my built-in babysitter. I adored her, forever identifying her with the lovely platinum-and-gold teddy bear she gave me for my first birthday. Being the first of his kind to enter my life, I never knew what it was to be without Teddy. Early on, relatives discovered that giving me dolls was only partially successful. Stuffed animals and birds were what I really cared for.

In the autumn of 1933, after Dad received his Bachelor of Arts degree in English, we moved to Kansas City. A teaching job for both Dad and Mum! Even if it did last only nine months, that was almost prosperity for the "Dirty Thirties," as those Depression years were called.

We lived in three rooms at the back of the schoolhouse. Every weekday I had all the kids, big and small, to play with. I had no idea that I was undergoing the privations of an "only child." We walked to church every weekend. In fact, we walked everywhere, except for long adventures down into the city when we used the streetcar. The most interesting events I knew about seemed to be connected with church. The pastor had three boys who went to our school. I admired them very much and thought they had a funny name, Lickey.

One of the church deacons had a cookie factory near the school, and he made it worthwhile visiting there. But after he committed suicide we couldn't get any more cookies. I really couldn't figure out what had gone wrong. Most of the rest of church would have been tiresome, but Mum always kept me busy with crayons and paper, so I didn't mind.

I never really understood why we spent the summers with Grandpa and Grandma Rhoads in Chariton, Iowa. Certainly I enjoyed the train journey, and I loved the warm, dusty days there, playing in the asparagus patch and swinging under the big elm trees by the front gate. Not once did I wonder why we went to the same place every year. At age three-going-on-four one doesn't ask that kind of question.

Years later I would learn that for their very survival Dad and Mum had to go to Grandpa's house. Their paycheck dried up on the last day of school every spring. These frequent visits to Chariton made me a favorite grandchild for no better reason than that I was, in those earliest years, "at home" at Grandma's more than any of my cousins could be.

So Dad helped Grandpa in the big gardens. Not that he scorned working on the land, but he dreamed of research in quiet shadowy libraries, of poetry, painting and music, of exploring ideas with like-minded colleagues, of writing, and of traveling. More painful than the blisters on his hands, however, was the knowledge that he couldn't support his family without charity received from his in-laws.

He carried the searing scars of the Depression for the rest of his life. Indeed, he feared any kind of investment, even real estate. "I'd rather just sit down and look at my bank book in the evening," he would say in later years. "I just spent too much time walking the streets without even five cents in my pocket."

I am sure that at no time during the Kansas City years did Dad or Mum ever feel that their life had really "begun." For me, on the other hand, all of this *was* the beginning. Carefree as a grasshopper, I thought we lived in a vast and marvelous house, furnished daily with dozens of playmates. As for the summers, I couldn't have been happier if we'd taken a Mediterranean cruise every year. I'd never even seen the ocean yet, so what did I know?

# CHAPTER 2

# What Is a Wedding?

In the summers, away from the school, I could entertain myself happily enough among the adults. Still, while I co-existed with them, a great many things puzzled me. Even so, I seldom asked questions. I liked the challenge of working out problems for myself.

Sometimes Auntie Middy came home to Chariton from her teaching job in south Nebraska. She and I were great friends. She arrived in her bright green 1932 Chrysler, the first car I could remember ever riding in. I'd sit in the rumble seat in an absolute frenzy of joy with the wind tearing through my bobbed hair.

Auntie Middy added some other dimensions to my small life also. Indeed, the first time I'd tasted ice cream was during one of her Chariton visits. The neighbors, the Belkey family, came over with their crank freezer to make a party. I padded softly downstairs in my pajamas to watch. By special dispensation Mum had allowed me to stay up late and be at the party. That is, to join in the sacred rite of eating ice cream. No one I knew even owned a refrigerator, so that night I savored a truly high moment. More was to come.

In the spring of 1934, Auntie Middy came home with a handsome young man. I heard that Wilbur Bennett was learning to be a doctor. At first I tried to ignore the stranger because no one I knew ever seemed to want to go see the doctor. Yet, since he didn't do any of the "doctor stuff," I decided to like him. Especially when he tickled me and tossed me in the air. The most astonishing thing, however, was when he lay back on the couch, and Aunt Middy poured a whole pitcher of water down his throat, non-stop. After that, I came near worshipping him because I'd never seen anyone that smart before.

Then, suddenly, everyone was getting ready for the wedding.

I'd never been to a wedding before, but I knew that it somehow involved my beloved Auntie Middy and that afterwards I would call the wonderful water-drinker "Uncle Wilbur." Instinctively, I knew that everyone was very busy, and I tried hard to keep out of the way.

Finally, a preacher came right to Grandma's little living room, and he did the wedding there. Aunt Middy stood very slim and tall in her lovely new blue dress with the bouncy hemline. "But she's taller than he is!" The preacher's wife whispered to one of the neighbors. I couldn't see what difference that made. I didn't like her much anyway, so I turned my back on her and concentrated on the people standing in the archway to the tiny piano room. Grandma was crying, but she cried a lot anyway. So that didn't bother me either.

When it was all over, everyone sat down, and I still didn't know what a wedding was. I knew that it must have already happened. Since I didn't feel any different, I worried that I must have missed something.

Next came the food. Mum pushed my little stool up to the old black Windsor chair that I'd been sitting on. I sat expectantly while she tied on my bib. "Now, Dottie, you can use the seat of the chair for your table. And don't … ," she tossed back as she hurried away, "don't spill anything on your new dress."

I knew a big white cake would come out by and by. I'd seen it in the downstairs kitchen that morning. In fact, I'd tested the thickness of the frosting with one finger, just to be sure it was real. We never had much cake. It wasn't supposed to be good

**Marriage of Wilbur Bennett and Mildred Rhoads, Chariton, Iowa.**

for us. I never could figure out, though, why something that everyone enjoyed so much had to be bad.

Mum set a large wedge of cake in front of me. Looking around, I saw to my surprise that mine was as big as anyone else's. Surely, someone had made a mistake! I watched the cake carefully and said nothing, hoping no one would notice. Then Grandma put my cereal bowl down on the seat of the chair. In it was … ice cream! I almost wept for the excitement of it all.

The bowl had a broad, flat bottom to accommodate a thick square of ice cream. The glory of it all was that it had three colors! I'd never realized before that ice cream could be anything but white. In a fever of ecstasy I looked at the stripes—pink, white and chocolate brown.

I still didn't know what a wedding was. But now, because I had the cake and ice cream, it didn't seem so important any more.

Then someone asked the minister to return thanks. How could they, with the tri-colored ice cream there in front of them! How could anyone close his eyes? The preacher stood up, in no hurry at all, and began to say a long grace over the food. Of course, I knew you had to close your eyes for blessing. My hot little fists clenched over my bib, I squeezed my eyes shut.

But the agonizing darkness cut me off from my ice cream. I took one tiny peep. It was still there. I forced my eyelids shut again but only for a moment. What if the vision should vanish while I wasn't watching? The minister droned on as if he had to bless food for all of the next week as well.

I decided I just couldn't risk not guarding my ice cream. I leaned forward, nose almost in the dish and watched the

In later years, **Mildred Bennett took Dorothy to see the old house where the family lived together in Lincoln, Nebraska (1931). There her Aunt Mid became her first (very enthusiastic) babysitter.**

smooth, creamy melt begin around the edges of the rainbow slab. Then I studied the worn back-panel of the chair and the little perforations in the seat of the chair. But I didn't close my eyes again. I couldn't.

That was, I think, the first time I'd dared to keep my eyes open during prayer. My desire for the ice cream completely overrode any guilt I might have felt. God would simply have to understand!

Finally, the preacher wound down, and we could get on with the eating.

I dipped my spoon into the pink ice cream first. A magnificent moment! One to be shared, surely! Forgetting the cake, I picked up my bowl of ice cream. I went to Auntie Middy and set my dish on her lap. She and my new uncle smiled at me, and we all ate together. Complete bliss in this sacred communion where I had ice cream and someone loving me too.

At last I understood what a wedding was. I didn't have to ask because now I knew.

# CHAPTER 3

# On Being an Invalid

Late one Friday afternoon I sat in the big galvanized washtub in the kitchen. I enjoyed bath-time, probably because it came only once a week. The stage setting required a lot of work on Mum's part. She carried the water into the kitchen, heated it on the cook stove and then hauled me in from the dirt bank behind the school. I was the chief participant in this regular Friday ceremony. On the other days she scrubbed me every night from a basin. Compared with this luxuriating in the laundry tub, the other washings were simply annoying.

So I sat there lolling in the suds. Then I looked down and saw a peculiar spot on my tummy. "Look, Mum! What's this?"

She hurried over to inspect the abnormality and became, I thought, unnecessarily excited about it. After all, it wasn't causing me any inconvenience.

By the next morning, however, I found myself somewhat inconvenienced with a magnificent case of chicken-pox, blossomed out from crown to toe. While I don't suppose that I felt well, I can't remember feeling sick either. Neither then nor in the episode which followed.

The chicken pox itself would have been uneventful had it not been followed by a heart complication with a long name. Suddenly, in our tiny three-room apartment we became crowded by the presence of a doctor who came to visit daily. Not feeling sick at all, I resented the man roundly. He was the one who announced that I must stay in bed, immobilized at all times. Not even my head raised by a pillow. He scared Mum and Dad by telling them that if they were not very strict with me I'd be an invalid the rest of my life. "She would likely die quite young," he murmured. So they were strict.

At first I found it a novelty eating in bed. Also, my meager supply of toys and books began multiplying around me. On the morning of my fourth birthday the mailman delivered two packages to our door. They contained two identical chocolate-brown teddy bears, mailed from opposite sides of the country. Then I got a silly dog, parti-colored yellow and black. He sat on his rump more like a teddy bear than a dog. For want of a better name, I just called him Dog. A number of other fuzzy creatures entered my life at this time, though the original Gold Teddy Bear remained the king of them all.

Soon parents of the school children and people from the church brought me families of small china animals, all "Made in Japan." Although I didn't know where Japan was, I immediately wanted to go there because obviously it was full of animals.

Occasionally one or two of the school kids would come in to help me play with the little porcelain figures. Tinker-toys and blocks made pens and barns in the hills and valleys of the bedclothes. There a herd of glossy green elephants dwelt domestically with half a dozen black-and-white cats and some blue dogs. My favorite family was a proud, multicolored rooster with his mild, modest white hen and three fat yellow chicks with beady black eyes. A curvaceous swan ran a close second, but she wasn't as round and comfortable to hold in the hands as were the hen and chicks.

Since I was confined to bed, the basic games I played with the animals were "School" and "Church." They were sedentary, and I knew more about those activities than any other. I alternated the long hours supervising the animals with reading books. Actually, I couldn't read much, but I studied the pictures in their minutest details. I invented fantastic stories to go with the pictures, most of them marvelous adventures in which I was always a living, breathing heroine who never had to go to bed. The last point was the punch line of every story.

No quantity of books or toys, however, helped my real difficulty. I was hopelessly cut off from the main stream of life. Not a very responsible life yet, to be sure. Still, it was mine, and I was always busy. Although I had no malicious intent to disobedience, staying flat in bed was so hard. School life continued to swirl about my little island of sickness, always within sight and sound, but just out of my reach.

Every morning Dad carried me out to the living room and laid me on the ragged old daybed under the window, just so I could have a little change of scenery for the long hours ahead. He and Mum then took turns rushing between classrooms and apartment to be sure that I was still lying down. The sound of the children romping in the schoolyard at recess, however, often proved to be too much. Cautiously, I'd sit up on my little couch just to peer over the windowsill. Then, fascinated with all the activity, I'd kneel up and press my nose to the windowpane—only to be snatched from behind and laid down flat again when an adult came into the room.

The policing of my convalescence obviously created difficulties. First, Big Uncle John Spriggs and Aunt Blanche (Grandpa's sister) came for a while. Both nurses, they managed me very well for the time they were there. I tended to talk non-stop whenever I had company with me. Fortunately, the doctor hadn't said that talk would weaken my heart. A good thing, for it was one of the few outlets I had. I might well have worn out Aunt Blanche, but hers was a long-lived family. In fact, she lived into her 103rd year, so I must not have done her any great harm.

Next, Grandpa and Grandma came down from Chariton to manage my

An appointed "team" supervised Dorothy during her long illness. In addition to Mum, Dad, and helpful friends, others came to work in shifts. That is, to be sure that she did not sit up on her bed. *Left:* Grandpa Bert and Grandma Mary Rhoads. *Above:* Aunt Blanche (Rhoads) and Uncle John Spriggs.

sick room. My body immobilized on the bed, my mind took wild flights into fantasy, and I filled Grandma's ears with outrageous tales and nonsensical ideas all day long. In between times, Grandpa started me off an a marvelous journey around the world. Geography, history and excitement all came in one glorious package. I entered into the expedition so wholeheartedly that I really expected us to leave on the trip tomorrow, if not yet tonight. Sometimes Grandma feared that Grandpa's imaginings were getting to be too potent. Yet Grandpa and I toured the world in a joyful safari without ever once disobeying the doctor's orders. Ironically, my later life did encompass a great part of the itinerary that my Grandpa laid out for me.

So the weeks stretched into months, and the fall into winter. The doctor kept coming twice a week. I suppose I could have been nice to him and been happier, but I identified him as the cause of my imprisonment. Besides, if he'd really liked children, he would have known how to break through my four-year-old frustrations.

At last, the moment came when that remote personage, the doctor, proclaimed, "Let her try walking today."

I stiffened to attention. Walk? What did he mean try. Just let me up and at it. I swung my legs off the old daybed and bounced to the floor. I staggered two steps forward and collapsed into Dad's arms. When I discovered that I couldn't walk, my confidence drained away like stale soup down the sink. I burst into tears. I'd waited so long.

Mum and Dad took turns holding me and comforting me. Somewhere in the confusion the doctor walked out of my life. I know that I had to go and see him for check-ups afterwards, but once I'd learned how to walk again, he simply didn't count any more. I remember nothing of those subsequent visits. Be it said to his credit and to the vigilance of my family, however, my heart condition completely righted itself. I still wonder if three months in bed was the only possible cure.Back then I felt as if I had lost half a lifetime!

# CHAPTER 4

# The Doughnuts

Being perpetually the "littlest one" was not consistently advantageous. Too often I fell adrift in a sea of adult concerns far beyond my comprehension. A Halloween party given by some of the school mothers turned out to be a case in point.

It must have been the first real party I'd ever attended. The house had a real lawn in front and an awesome double front door. I took a firmer grip on my mother's hand as we stepped through onto a real (I think Persian) carpet. Inside, table lamps discreetly highlighted dark, polished woods. I'd never seen this world before.

When we reached the dining room, I saw a chandelier blazing over a huge round table. Orange-and-black paper chains festooned the ceiling and several jack-o-lanterns peered wickedly out from the dry cornstalks standing in the middle of the white damask tablecloth.

I sat between Patty Ann, my favorite third-grader, and Joey Simms. Surely my cup overflowed! A party with the big kids! One marvel after another issued forth from the kitchen. I'd never seen such food! Little sandwiches made out of white store-bought bread. Shiny tarts with crinkly edges. Apples wearing sticky toffee coats. My head swam with the immensity of the possibilities before me.

Then came the grand climax, an absolutely gigantic platter of doughnuts. The fat, bumpy glazed rings glistened in the jack-o-lantern light, a pyramid of gooey perfection. I fairly ached with pleasure as I reached, both hands, for a doughnut.

The feast, however, took on sudden moral implications when the doughnut platter came by the second time. I'd already eaten above and beyond the range of my wildest imaginations. I began to wonder if I really had a duty to stop, simply because at our house everything was done with discipline and moderation.

Everyone around me took more doughnuts. "Go ahead." Patty saw my hesitation. "Your mother won't mind." She spoke with difficulty because her mouth was full of doughnut.

"Yeah," Joey affirmed, a doughnut in each hand. 'These are the best ever." I looked around for Mum, but she was nowhere to be seen. I felt that I couldn't take another doughnut without asking permission. I really hadn't made that kind of a decision before. I choked back the tears as the platter went by.

Presently the doughnuts came by a third time. Now strengthened in my sense of virtue, I again refused them. Patty Ann and Joey stared at me in amazement. " Well then, you ought to go and ask your mother." Patty advised.

Dorothy and her Dad in the schoolyard on Monroe Street, Kansas City. The family lived in three small rooms at the back of the schoolhouse.

Christmas 1934 brought Dorothy a brand new tricycle, the most magnificent gift she had received up to that time. It even tempered the misery caused by those loathsome cotton stockings she had to wear.

I agonized with my problem, praying that Mum would come into view so that I could request a special dispensation on the doughnuts. She didn't appear. To climb down from my chair and go to hunt for her in the big, strange house was unthinkable.

So I sat, a model of ascetic sobriety, among all the exuberant, uninhibited children. As I watched the doughnut orgy go on, my zest for the parry waned. I just couldn't cope with the inner taskmaster who'd somehow forbidden my having more than one doughnut. My compensation, however, was a rather euphoric but undefined sense of having "done right."

Finally, the parry ended, and Mum and I walked home. Obediently I trotted down the sidewalk, my hand in hers. In a warm glow of satisfaction, I told her about the doughnuts. "And I had only one because I thought you wouldn't want me to have any more."

I looked up expectantly, awaiting her approval. "Oh, Dottie," she said, "you could have had more than one. It was a party, after all."

I froze where I stood. Paralyzed I looked down at the cracks in the sidewalk, where they spidered out to the schoolyard fence. I never knew there could be such keen disappointment in all the world. Such bleak regret. Such sheer misery.

In effect, my life ended right there on the sidewalk. Having lost those doughnuts, I didn't see how the future could possibly hold any more joy for me. Indeed, in my broken little four-year-old heart, I felt a stab of pain akin to that of a sinner who has just discovered that he's lost heaven. And to think that I got it from trying to be good!

My sense of righteousness gave way to abject despair as Mum, all unaware of the tragedy she'd caused, dragged me up the front steps into our apartment behind the schoolhouse.

Even the most sensitive adults seldom realize when these tragedies occur. Life has so many other bigger problems for them. Nonetheless, I couldn't talk about my grief. I could only brood over it, feeling such a great emptiness inside that not even tears would come. To this day, I never see a doughnut without feeling the shadow of that day pass over me anew.

The doughnut affair, however, marked the beginning of my moral decline. Up to that time, I'd never thought of transgressing Mum's law about never eating between meals. A few days later, at recess time, one of the kids offered me a piece of hard, pink candy, I took it. I did not save it. Instead, I ate it on the spot.

When fire did not fall from heaven and consume me, I heaved a sigh of relief. I could eat something in the middle of the morning and still live! From that day onward my whole theology of food changed.

# CHAPTER 5

# The Good Eggs

That summer when I was four-years-old-going-on-five we went, as usual, to Grandpa and Grandma's tiny homestead-house in Chariton, Iowa. Of all the new experiences that that annual excursion opened up to a city-bred child like me, the affairs in the chicken yard were by far the most interesting.

Now my attitudes toward chickens remain ambivalent to this day. They are serviceable, harmless creatures, and certainly I have never wished them any ill. On the other hand, they have always struck me as singularly stupid and foolish, possibly the most witless of all God's birds and beasts.

From the beginning of my adventures in the hen house, I was somehow fascinated by the interminable scratching, the vulgar cackling and the flapping

**Dorothy within Grandpa Rhoads' chicken yard, Chariton, Iowa—on one of her good days when she did *not* chase the hens.**

about in the roosts. I took inordinate delight in creating little disturbances among those simple-minded birds, just for the pleasure of seeing them explode into a panic of feathers and squawks.

The presence of Grandpa, however, would always encourage my more mature instincts. I soberly accompanied him on the daily rounds, searching each nesting box for eggs, Henny Penny's little white ones, the big, buff-brown offerings of Biddy McCorkle, and all the rest.

I also took my responsibility very seriously when I carried the egg basket in to Grandma. It gave me a sense of participation and ownership in the tasty dishes that came from the old wood stove to the big round table down in the summer kitchen. I sat at my place at the worn oilcloth, feeling as much a sense of proprietorship as any other lady in the house. The egg gathering really did enhance my self-esteem.

Indeed, I discharged my duties with such distinction that by the third day of summer vacation that year I was making the egg rounds all by myself. It was then that I discovered that some perverse hens chose not to lay their eggs in the nesting boxes. Every day I found three or four stray eggs under the hen house, beside the water trough, or in the dusty hollows under the scrubby bushes.

Although I had received no special instruction concerning those mis-placed eggs, I assumed that an egg not laid in the proper place was not a good egg. All of those, I supposed, were mine to dispose of as I saw fit.

They made a very pleasant splat when I threw them against the side of the hen house. Broken shells mixed with the bright yellow yolks and flowed down onto the ground. In rapture, the hens began eating their own eggs. The sound of a breaking egg aroused a most satisfying rush of activity. The excited fowls raced from all over the chicken yard to gobble up the golden stream. As they croaked and trampled over one another, I'd laugh until I cried.

Thus, egg production had fallen off appreciably by the time my father discovered my self-imposed methods of egg sorting. Immediately, the admin-istration of the hen house passed back into adult hands.

For two weeks I was banned from the chicken yard. So I sat under the raspberry bushes and watched the idiot hens twittering about on the other side of the fence. By running up and down along the barricade, however, I could still stir up a lot of activity. I loved the way the half-crazed birds would rush through the yard, cackling and flapping until they dropped.

Once again the egg-laying count went down. I'd been under surveillance only a day or two when even this recreation was also denied to me. I was promptly excluded from the raspberry patch as well.

At the end of the month, however, I made such a convincing show of repentance that I could return to my original status, making the rounds with Grandpa.

Yet, I think I was charged with far more malice than I was guilty of in this matter. Although they may have been a little over-exercised, the chickens themselves did enjoy eating their eggs and probably had never been happier in their lives. The adult government of the house, however, thwarted the entire enterprise.

"But if the eggs weren't in the nests," I wailed through my stormy tears of frustration, "I didn't think they were any good!"

# CHAPTER 6

# Monday's Child

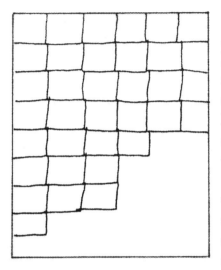

I never could figure out dropouts. Surely going to school had to be one of life's most obvious and pleasurable routines. It just didn't occur to me that any one would contemplate not finishing high school. Or, having done that, that he or she could have any plan in mind other than going on to college.

When, at length, I discovered this viewpoint to be highly visionary, I sometimes wondered how I'd come to be that odd child who always preferred books above all other diversions. The one who greeted Monday mornings with the zest most people reserve for Saturday nights and bank holidays.

Obviously, it all has to go back to that schoolhouse in Kansas City. Actually, I have no recollection of ever beginning school. For me there was no coming home to announce that I'd assimilated the total sum of knowledge in my first week of school. No great "first day" to be feared and anticipated. No mighty rite of passage to propel me from pre-school into school proper. Somehow I always just seemed to be there. The classroom became as natural a habitat for me as my bed.

Because Mum had no special training for teaching, Dad was her mentor in those years. Years that would no doubt have been easier for them without me. Day-care centers and baby-sitters were not even words in the vocabulary yet. Even if they had been, my parents wouldn't have had five cents to pay for the service. After hours of administering arithmetic, geography and justice, Dad came back to the apartment in the evening to clean house and help Mum with lesson plans. She came back to our washing, ironing and cooking.

Where did I fit in? I just went to school. What else?

Actually, I suppose I really was on the perimeter of things, but I felt thor-

**Dorothy was genetically programmed for a bookish life, as the future careers of both her parents demonstrated. Left: Gerald Minchin classified his personal library according to the Dewey Decimal library system. Center: He lived by his typewriters and never left home without his little portable model. Right: As an executive secretary, Leona Minchin mastered, among other things, the duplicating machine that preceded today's copiers.**

oughly involved. Patty Ann always helped me drag my sled up the snowy hill in the back yard. I joined most of the big girls in Grades 3 and 4 when they huddled together in private little corners telling girl-secrets. Above all, there was a little table just for me, set beside the Grade I row of desks. From there I followed as much of the storytelling as I liked and spent the rest of the time drawing tigers in brilliant green jungles or modeling little men out of pink plasticine (modeling clay) and giving them acorn caps.

One odd little exercise I invented for myself was using tracing paper over lined tablet paper to create hundreds of squares. Sometimes I'd fill in a design, but often just a stark page full of squares gave me great satisfaction. The product was important enough to me that every once in a while I'd have Mum send a page of squares off to Grandpa and Grandma. I never failed to get a reply commending me lavishly on the excellence of my performance. I still don't know what I did them for.

It was fortunate for Mum and Dad that I took so agreeably to the classroom. If I hadn't, they would have had some major problems. As it was, I just sat there and learning seeped through my pores. By the time I was five I could read just about any kids book in Mum's classroom. Just how and when the thing happened, I have no idea.

What really restored me after my long bout with rheumatic fever was school and all of my friends in it. The day I returned to my little table in the schoolroom, I just knew I'd come home. By the time early spring came, I was one of the first to fall off the teeter-totter and tear the knees out of my loathsome brown stockings that blighted all of my winters. I suffered the pain gladly, for it released me into the barefoot joys of summer a little early. No more heart trouble for me!

One winter, however, I got a terrible case of whooping cough. I coughed in season and out. Believing that in some way the stockings would help, poor Mum mended the knees and kept the stockings on me anyhow. Several kids at school had whooping cough too and had, apparently, to wear their stockings for the same reason. So, we all whooped and hacked and honked for weeks until we wore out everyone, including ourselves. Then, sure enough, with the coming of warm weather, we all got better.

Compared with what Mum and Dad had, I reared my own two children under optimum conditions, I think. For my parents, indeed, there existed virtually no line of demarcation between the private and the public, home and school. Emotionally, physically, and spiritually life rolled on as one single, overwhelming unit there on Monroe Street.

Eventually, my husband and I lived in a house separate from the school. Also, we had a car and could more or less come and go as we wished. Moreover, we got paid every month of the year.

Nonetheless, one worthwhile benefit accrued from the Kansas City phase of our lives. That experience set me up academically for my whole life. I've always loved school and have never been happier than when I am in the classroom, on one side of the desk or the other. Or, better still, in a library.

# CHAPTER 7

# Enduring the Depression

There were additional stringencies brought on by the Depression, other than our going to Chariton every summer. Throughout the Kansas City winters Mum took in extra washing and ironing. She did it at night, after a full day in the classroom teaching Grades 1 to 4. Dad sold the free-lance articles he wrote in the evenings after he'd worked all day teaching Grades 5 to 8. I made extra work for both of them, though I was conditioned to a strict and early bedtime.

Reasons for that extra labor probably went beyond just my health. Mum always made our bread, of course. Sometimes, though, we had trouble about clothes. At first, I knew nothing of store-bought clothes. Grandmas were the only source of clothing that I knew of. Mine made me a blue coat with silk lining and a matching bonnet. Because I had a congenital dislike for hats, the coat gave me more joy than did the bonnet. Every dress Grandma made me had matching bloomers. Only after I found that the First Grade girls in Kansas City wore "boughten" panties made of silky rayon, did my bloomers become a vexation of spirit to me. Had I realized that I'd be wearing that sturdy homemade lingerie for the next five years, I might well have been quite discouraged.

Moreover, I bore another more onerous burden. It didn't come directly as a result of the Depression, although I did wonder if rich girls had to wear them too. It was a curse that went with winter weather. At that time, snow-suits and jeans had not yet been invented for small females. It was the dreadful harness that Mum used to suspend my coarse brown cotton stockings from my shoulders. Almost every morning, the complication of getting me dressed brought me to tears. Once on my small frame, the nefarious device bound my whole torso in a nagging network of straps and bands. All of this on top of the homemade underwear! Moreover, Mum, for whatever reasons, tended to keep me in the odious stockings halfway through the summer.

I believed that Grandma's new White sewing machine could do anything. Apparently Grandpa had faith in her sewing-room magic too. He'd bring home little remnants of fabric, confident that she could make a dress out of a piece, even if it were but half a yard. Indeed, Grandma did do marvels, using every last scrap in the quilts that are now family heirlooms. Feed sacks made aprons and pajamas. Then there were always enough bits of everything left over to make jackets and pants for my teddy bears.

In a bid, perhaps, to make me care for dolls at least as much as animals, the family put a beautiful doll under the Christmas tree for me one year. With a fine bisque face under her dark curls and the daintiest of hands and feet, my Rosebud was very lovely, to be sure. Grandma had made her a dress with tiny pink rosebuds, pink bows, and, naturally, matching bloomers. I loved her, of course. Who wouldn't? I did so, however, in the respectful way one reserves for powerful people and dowager queens. The doll never could, in all the years of her long life, replace the comfort of the Golden Teddy nestled in my arms.

I thought our Kansas City apartment quite spacious for all of our needs. A dresser, double bed, and my little cot completely filled the tiny bedroom, leaving only an eight-inch walkway between the beds. The windows on two sides filtered warm sunbeams through ruffled white marquisette curtains. Mum always had the artistic touch.

Grandpa Rhoads pedaled his garden produce around Chariton, often with Dorothy going along for the ride, sitting atop the vegetables. Here they exchanged ends of the wheelbarrow.

In the kitchen a tall, glossy enamel cupboard offset the worn spots in the linoleum and somehow lent the humble room a polished modern air. All my spills could easily be wiped up off the matching white enamel table. There I ate my graham crackers off my yellow plate with two dogs in the middle and assorted cats and ducks around the rim. I couldn't have imagined food served in anything else.

Above all, our home stood in the heart of a bustling schoolyard, and I loved it. Our living room had little in it except the daybed, a couple of chairs, and a desk. That was it!

The bathroom situation must have been trying for Mum and Dad. Not for me, of course. I had the warm comfort of the galvanized tub in the kitchen and a modest little green potty under my bed. My parents had to share facilities with all the school kids in the basement. Just keeping the place clean took hours out of their lives. Over a drain, near the tall, very loud toilet, Dad set up a bucket with holes punched in the bottom. He hung it from a big nail he'd hammered into a rafter. He always liked a shower, and his system did work.

Such is the power of happiness and contentment in a family. I never knew we were poor. For a long time I didn't think there was anyone else in the world who had things better than we did.

Our frugalities, of course, went on all summer at Grandpa's house too. It's just that in the warm weather, I suppose there were fewer things to worry about. Mum and Auntie Mid sold Watkins essences and flavorings from door to door. Sometimes they made delicious sour-cream prune cakes (after their Grandma Rowland's recipe) and sold them too.

Grandpa always had a big vegetable garden. He cultivated all the land around his house and then rented a large field from Mr. Fuller, over by the railway tracks. The womenfolk canned everything that could be sealed into a bottle. We ate bountifully at the table, and still we had enough produce to fill a warehouse. Grandpa would load up his wheelbarrow and trudge up and down the streets of Chariton selling vegetables. I sat on the potatoes at the front of the barrow. I loved those early sunny mornings, especially when we came to the big house with gargoyles on the gateposts.

"And I think I'd like to have this little girl too," a housewife sometimes said after her beets, asparagus, carrots had been put in her basket. "How much will she cost?"

Grandpa would always stand back and look down at me as if he were debating a price and then say. "Well, she isn't for sale this morning. We've just decided to keep her for display." After the first few times, I could relax. Grandpa never told a lie, so I knew that I didn't have to worry. They planned to keep me.

One summer, when Mum's brother, James Rhoads and his family also lived in Chariton, I had a chance to get acquainted with my cousins, Berton and Gayle. One was a year older and the other a year younger than I. It reminded me, in a limited way, of recess time in Kansas City.

For just three little kids, we managed to create some trouble for ourselves. One day we all decided to go to college. Fair enough. Then it was decided that I should see a doctor before I went. (If only we'd known, this is about the time I ought to have seen a real eye doctor and been put into glasses.) Berton volunteered as doctor and treated my eyes with dead leaves and twigs.

Bert Rhoads reconstructed a very livable house atop what had been the town dump in Chariton, Iowa. In 1936, the family gathered together for a last visit before the embarkation of part of the family to Singapore and Borneo. Seated in front: Grandma Mary Rhoads. Standing, from left: Bert Rhoads, Mildred Bennett, Gerald Minchin, Leona Minchin, and Norma Youngberg, holding Ben. At the back, from left: Dorothy Minchin, Madge Youngberg, and Jimmy Youngberg.

He did it with the same meticulous care that he would give to his work later when he grew up. (He became a historian and Chief of the National Archives of the United States.)

Because of Berton's malpractice I then had to see a real doctor for an eye infection. About the same time, we got too boisterous with our tire-swing, and Gayle fell out of it and broke his nose.

A short time later came the decree that I had to have my tonsils removed. Too young to have much idea about what it was all about, I went off to the clinic happy enough. Because I had a promise of all the ice cream I wanted to eat afterwards, nothing else mattered.

I took a dislike to the doctor though. He clamped the ether mask over my face and held my arms down, violently. Actually, the operation was an ill starred event. The doctor turned out to be an alcoholic. (He committed suicide two weeks later.) This fact was not public knowledge at the time of my operation, of course, or Mum and Dad would certainly have looked elsewhere. Even more inconvenient to me than the doctor's death was the fact that my tonsils grew back again. I had recurring infections for years to come.

Hard times maybe, but I remember a steady stream of guests at Grandpa and Grandma's table. Perhaps their times were even harder than ours. Some of them almost looked like hobos out of the railway yards. One old man had a startling white beard and prayed long prayers over the food. I thought he must be near to God. I don't remember how or why I started calling him "Anee."

Then old Elder Hawkins used to come by. He probably had a more profound effect on Auntie Mid than on me. He held a belief upon which he expounded loudly and at length. "Don't ever have any children," he would advise the dinner-table company. "They are all from the Devil."

Since I was the only child in the household, it was obvious to whom he was referring. I wondered if it included just me or my Gold Teddy too. Auntie Middy always believed in me and teddies as well. Once she got so angry that she left the table because of what Elder Hawkins said.

There are more kinds of Depression than just one, I discovered that day.

# CHAPTER 8

# It is More Blessed

Shortly after my fourth birthday, the enterprising leaders of the church ladies group devised a Christmas program. It was scheduled to be performed before the whole church on a frosty December evening. The highlight of the event was to be a manger scene to which all of the children would go, each in purest childish innocence, bearing a gift of one of his or her toys. These gifts, we understood, were to be sent to needy children in faraway places. After this beautiful act of unselfishness, we were all to lift our generous little hearts in the singing of "Silent Night."

Since I'd never had a great surplus of toys, the question of giving up anything I possessed was a searching one indeed. Carefully I examined my family of teddy-bears and stuffed dogs, but I couldn't consider parting with even the least of them. The doll Rosebud was far too lovely and sophisticated even to be considered. What to do? Really, it seemed too much to ask!

Then my eye fell upon the smooth, rotund form of the Cream of Wheat Man. I'd never cared for him from the day he came in the mail. Mum had ordered him as a premium with the purchase of the cereal. I liked Cream of Wheat, but I'd never liked him. Naturally, then, he would be the one to go.

In passing, I wondered if this was what it meant to make a sacrifice for the poor children of India, as we'd been admonished. Or was it Africa? Should it have been my dearest Gold Teddy? I couldn't tolerate that thought for an instant. No, the Man's fat white body and billowy chef's cap, I convinced myself, would look good at the manger.

Finally, the big night came. The program came off well, and I remembered all the lines of the piece I had to say. Or at least, most of them. The Welfare Room had been used for dressing, and there the ladies rushed about organizing the children for the grand finale, the manger scene. Being one of the smaller participants, I stood somewhere down near the end of the line of little pilgrims.

I looked into the painted pink face of the Cream of Wheat Man in my arms: Suddenly I wondered why I'd never loved him. I thought of the nights when I'd taken all my animals to bed with me, putting the most cherished one right next to me. The second best, next, and so forth, all in order of preference out to the far edges of the bed. Now I remembered that he'd never slept next to me, while all the others had had at least one turn. Indeed, I could remember that most of the time he'd slept on the floor under the bed.

Remorse flooded me in a terrible wave of guilt. Even today, I can scarcely remember having felt worse. I just knew I couldn't give him up. I had to take him home and make it up to him. Darting between the distracted teachers, I found a box of old clothes and plunged my newly beloved Man under them. My heart now burned with passion for him! I had to save him!

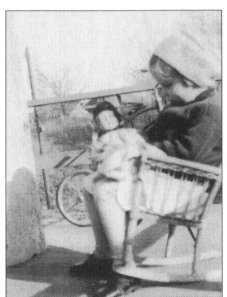

Dorothy respectfully accepted the only doll she ever received. Stuffed animals, however, remained her lifetime love.

Realizing that I was now physically unprepared to approach the manger, to say nothing of my spiritual frame of mind, I remained detached from the line of children. At that moment I cared nothing for the children of the world.

I hoped to be overlooked when the train of virtuous children moved on to the stage. In a moment, however, I was the center of attention with excited ladies and curious children swirling about me. Where was my gift? Why wasn't I in line? What about the starving children in India? Mum appeared somewhere out of the confusion. Normally, I would have been crying at this point. Instead, I fixed a tearless gaze upon her and flatly refused to reveal the whereabouts of the Cream of Wheat Man.

The anguish of the next few moments does not require detailed description. The pain of regret shredded my little heart to the core. Suffice to say that, with the help of some subtle bribery on my mother's part, I was persuaded to retrieve the Cream of Wheat Man and join the procession of more righteous children bound for the manger.

Why hadn't I loved him sooner? Nonetheless, if I hadn't given him up, someone else would have had to go. Who ever could that have been? Doing the right thing. Did it always have to hurt this much?

One can only hope that the subdued lighting of the stage partially hid the angry face of one rebellious gift-giver that night. Even now, decades later, the recollection of that wretched Christmas memory can still re-open the wound and make it bleed a little more.

# CHAPTER 9

# Keeping Ahead

By the time I was five my life had included a rather broad spectrum of experience. This, despite the fact that I hadn't been anywhere yet. Still, it was certainly all that I could handle at the time. Especially the car accident.

As little as we had to do with cars, it's surprising that it could have happened to us at all. But it did. Mum and Dad went to a midwinter teachers' convention in upstate Missouri. Instead of the usual train journey, we rode in Melvin Oss's car. He and Thelma McBroom were also teachers who had been bidden forth to the same convention. As usual, I went along as the mascot. Indeed, there was nowhere else for me to be.

Being allowed to take only one of my animal family, I'd chosen Dog, the yellow-and-black clown. One black ear and one yellow, one black leg and one black paw, and a half-black chest. Perhaps some premonition prompted me to leave the precious Gold Teddy and the twin chocolate-brown bears at home. So it was Dog who ventured out into the unknown with me.

While the meetings no doubt did my parents some good, for me the long ride in Mr. Oss's car was far and away the main feature. A car of early-thirties vintage had little to offer by way of space and convenience, though the real leather seats had to have counted for something. I nestled in the front seat between Dad's knees, next to the driver, and the two ladies sat in the back. I can remember being very cold, with the rain pelting bleakly against the square windows. Still, nothing, I thought, could diminish my enchantment with the simple joy of riding in a car that day.

Then it happened. Was automobile driving still such a novelty to everyone that it wasn't done well? Or was the weather that bad? Whatever it was, Mr. Oss should never have tried to pass another car on a hill, because there was a truck waiting for him just over the top.

Seeing the accident coming, Dad opened up his great woolen overcoat and yanked me inside it. When the crash came, I was held secure, close to his chest. Time stopped, and I froze in that warm darkness. I could feel his heart beating, fast.

After what seemed a long time Dad let my head come out into the light again. In an instant, our secure little world had exploded in a shower of flying glass and had landed in a heap of twisted metal. And the blood! Blood everywhere. The impact had wrenched Dog out of my arms, and now he lay in the back seat, soaked in blood too.

I don't remember how we got to the doctor's clinic. Suddenly, a lot of people surrounded us, and somehow we got in out of the cold. I saw Mum and Miss McBroom lying on two tables with a doctor and nurse working on them. Their glasses had been ground into their faces, and they had other big cuts from the non-shatter-proof window glass. Naturally, Dad and Mr. Oss were busy about them. Also, Dad had a twisted thumb. It bent out at a funny angle and had to be bandaged.

As for me, I huddled on the floor by the heater with poor Dog in my arms. "How fortunate that you could save her!" I heard someone say. "She isn't hurt at all."

But I was hurt, wounded in a deep place that no one could see. I believed that if a lot of blood came out of you, you died. Dog was so real to me that I thought he was bleeding to death. I sat quietly crying over his battered little body, great splotches of blood spattering

Now, more than seventy-five years later, Dog looks worn out with his many travels and with all of the love that has been poured on him. Nonetheless, he remains *alive*. Alive in his own special way. *(Photo by Cindy de Mille)*

his bright yellow-and-black coat. I didn't worry about the other people. The policeman and the doctor and nurses were all taking care of them. But no one paid any attention to Dog, and he'd soon be dead.

Then a nurse saw me. She came over, knelt beside me, and put her arms around me. "Dear little girl, are you hurting somewhere?"

"Yes." The tears came faster. "See? See?" I pulled away from her and held up Dog. "He's going to die, isn't he?" I burst into great heaving sobs.

"Oh, is this the trouble, then?" She seemed very young, even to me, but she was certainly very wise. "Well, you can help me, and we're going to make him all better."

She brought a basin of water and bathed him, the water running scarlet twice. The third time it came clean. Then she spread a little towel on top of the heater and laid Dog on it. He looked quite a bit thinner, and his fur stood up in wet tufts.

"Now I have other work to do," the nurse said. "But I want you to stay right here and watch him, because he's very tired. When he wakes up, he'll feel fine."

I took up my vigil over the convalescing Dog, contented but a little tired myself. It took a couple of hours for all the stitching and the application of bandages to be done to the other people. I suppose we went home to Kansas City on the train. I don't remember. The important thing was that I brought Dog home alive and well. As for Mum and Dad, I didn't have to worry about them. Parents are always there. They couldn't die anyway. Not the way Dog might have done.

I usually enjoyed the times when Dad got left alone with me. Nearly always something interesting happened. I liked the way he fumbled around doing domestic chores. For instance, if he couldn't get my harness sorted out (and usually he couldn't), he would be contented just leaving the wretched stockings off. Besides, he wasn't nearly as preoccupied with germs as Mum was. He never minded how much I played in the dirt.

Because he realized that Mum believed in it strongly, however, he knew that he had to be faithful about the castor oil. I was never clear about why I had to take it. Along with several other disgusting things, it fell under the rather vague heading of being "Good for Me." Sometimes, I noticed, it came into more prominence than others, but I never knew why or when. Capsules to contain castor oil hadn't yet been invented, so the treatment always involved a spoon, large as a garden shovel, full of the slimy, nauseous stuff. Mum had tried to camouflage it in orange or tomato juice. While I weathered through with the tomato, the procedure ruined my relationship with oranges for life.

One day Mum left Dad and me alone with three responsibilities: To change my clothes, to dose me with castor oil, and to meet her at the church. Mistakenly, he undertook the tasks in that order. First he got my red bloomers with the yellow roses on them and then put on the matching dress, backwards. (I didn't say anything because he was already having a hard time.) Then came the spoon of castor oil. I stood meekly before him, and down it went. I didn't mean to be rebellious, because I really liked doing things with Dad. Instantly and involuntarily, however, the process reversed and up it came, all over me, him, our shoes and the floor. "Jumping gingers!" he cried, dropping the spoon and leaping to his feet. I didn't mean to make him so nervous.

He said nothing more about taking castor oil, and for that I was properly thankful. Mum would never have abandoned the project, never until the goal was attained. Dad mopped things up as best he could, took off my dress and replaced it with the blue one with white daisies. Surprisingly, at that moment of crisis, his artistic sense didn't prompt him to correct the badly coordinated color scheme I now wore. Worse still, I carried the telltale taint of castor oil on my red bloomers the rest of the day. I can still, with great precision, recall the odor.

Our summers in Chariton could be every bit as educational as sitting in school with the Grade I kids. The Belkey boys from next door began conditioning me for going to Singapore where all the children on the mission compound would be boys. Occasionally, Grandma would let us play inside the house. Our favorite game, "Tiger," involved one of us covering up in the big tiger skin off Grandma's piano bench. The "It" crawled around on hands and knees making appropriate tiger noises while the rest of us screamed and climbed up on the furniture.

Generally, the party soon became too rough, and Grandma would order us outside. She'd lay the little stuffed crocodile across the doorway to watch us with his green glass eyes. We wouldn't dream of going back into the living room while he was there. Grandma was fortunate that she had these curios that Auntie Norma had sent back from the Far East. Unfortunately, one rather cancelled out the other. If she hadn't had that gorgeous Sumatran tiger skin, she wouldn't have needed the little crocodile so much.

More consistently interesting than either of the Belkey boys, however, was their mother. I'd never seen or heard anyone like her. Fern Belkey must have weighed in at 375 pounds at the least. Wheezing and gasping when she talked, she'd lumber over to sit on a creaking bench in Grandma's kitchen and visit. Also she had a peculiar speech defect that made her take a long time to tell a story.

With her eyes sunk into her face like two raisins in a white dumpling, she go on for an hour. I'd just sit at her feet to watch and listen. "And ya' know I haven't been well, huh (gasp) ... so I went to Davenport, huh, to see the doctor, huh (loud raspy cough). ... And heaven knows, huh, that I had this (gasp). . . .this terrible headache, huh. ... All that way on the train, huh, too (sigh). ... I just stood on my head all night, huh. It was that bad, huh, and would you believe, huh ... (wheez). "

Later on I heard someone say that the journey from Chariton to Davenport, Iowa was something like 200 miles. Remarkable! How did she do it?

Mrs. Belkey seemed to have an odd relationship with her mild little husband. I learned later that she'd have him taken off to jail whenever she felt he was drinking too much. Perhaps he got some rest there.

Anyway, she did try not to waste his money. One day she brought over some ice cream. Jubilant, I followed her into the house. She handed the bowl to Grandma. "(Sigh) Here ... (wheez), I, huh, thought ... huh ... you could (gasp) use this 'ere ice cream ... (sigh). I made a mistake, huh ... usin' salt 'stead a' suder (sugar) ... huh, but Ah didn't want ta waste, huh, all dem udder good suder an' aids (eggs), huh. So ... (gasp) ... you can eat it, huh."

Grandma graciously received the generous gift. After Mrs. Belkey finally heaved herself up and went home, Grandma dumped the ice cream down the outhouse hole. A sad waste, indeed, I thought!

I guess no one realized then, even Mrs. Belkey herself, that deafness was part of her problem. That's why, on Auntie Middy's wedding day, she rolled up to the front door with, "I cum, huh. . .(gasp). . .to graduate you." Also, she always told us how she made her applesauce from "Malicious" (Delicious) and "Ramsbolden" (Grimes Golden) apples.

Truly, Mrs. Belkey's visits were unfailingly memorable performances. Grandma and Mum would listen patiently. On the other hand, I, being a strict literalist, tried to visualize things like what did she look like after standing on her head all night. Or even after five minutes, for that matter.

Yes, my world was expanding. Then it burst wide open the day my Youngberg cousins arrived in Chariton.

# CHAPTER 10

# Working Out One's Salvation

In a1936 Dad and Mum accepted an overseas mission appointment to Singapore. The Youngbergs had come on home leave. They left their three older children in a boarding school in Idaho, and Uncle Gus returned to Borneo. Auntie Norma and the three younger ones, Madge, Jimmy, and Ben, came to spend part of the summer in Chariton.

Then, together, they and we would make the month-long ship crossing to the Orient.

When they first arrived, we spent the first day just looking at one another without saying a word.

While I had the advantage of being "on location" first, they numbered three and had the unity and clout that came with having a strong, recognized leader, Madge. Having cased out one another in silent speculation, we finally began communicating. Or, more correctly, I was adjudged worthy of being incorporated into the system. The breakthrough turned out to be sudden and complete.

We kids played for hours in the garden, until Grandpa barred us from the asparagus patch. We'd built so many clubhouses in there that by the time he discovered the carnage he hardly had any crop left. Then we turned to the flowerbeds. One morning, as we all sat under the rose bushes, Madge told us that we could just as well eat some dirt. "You know," she said, "you have to eat a peck of dirt before you die."

She almost persuaded me—but not quite—that I should start in order to get my quota of dirt in before time ran out. Jimmy ate a little, though. Four-year-old Ben ate an angleworm. It caused a little ripple of approval and astonishment that seemed to please him. I'd never before realized that eating could have powerful political and social uses. More was to come. Furthermore,

I'd never before had a chance to get so dirty. I loved it!

Playing with my cousins brought me both freedom and bondage, at the same time. Now, I had acquired a special identity apart from the adults around me. I became a bona fide member of the "Club of Grandchildren," the juveniles of the family. Never again would I be a single child in an adult world, Now I had my own context.

Once arrived in Singapore, the cousins had to wear regulation *topees* (sun helmets). From left: Nancy, Dorothy Minchin, Jimmy and Madge Youngberg.

Concurrently with this liberation, I fell into that powerful magnetic field which was Madge. Six years older than I, she had absolute power over her younger brothers and me—body, mind and soul. No feudal lord ever received more willing obedience.

My first attempt to fulfill my new role, however, almost killed me. We'd said goodbye to Grandpa and Grandma in Chariton, amid many tears. Tears on the part of others—certainly not us kids. I couldn't know how long a time seven years of absence would be. Next we stopped in Watertown for Auntie Norma and Mum to visit their brother James. Temporarily, this occasion added **Berton and Gayle to our group. The six of us made quite a pack!**

On our last evening Uncle Jimmy and Aunt Mary opened their rambling Victorian house to friends and neighbors for a farewell, send-off supper. Always there was good food, but several big, thumping-sweet watermelons constituted the main attraction.

Ever since the doughnut episode, I'd become more relaxed about food. I would secretly eat between meals. This evening wasn't the time. The tables were set up out on the lawn, a huge variety of food there for the taking. No adult supervision. We kids, therefore, interspersed our eating with playing games and climbing trees. Since no one paid any attention to us, we'd swing past the table and grab food, like railway-men hooking the bags of mail onto a moving train. I have no idea how many pieces of watermelon I ate. It tasted very good, and I put away a lot of it, along with a lot of other things as well.

Late that night I awoke, very sick. I know I'd never felt so bad before. I wondered if this is what dying was like. I ruined Mum's night and Aunt Mary's too, as they both stood by me every time I vomited. I went on vomiting long after every scrap of food was gone.

When we left on the train for Seattle the next day, I still felt green and quiet. Never again would I be able to come to terms with a piece of watermelon. A pity, because I came to find that not liking watermelon carries a stigma with it. People in that condition usually aren't considered normal.

Freedom, I was beginning to understand, has its price.

We spent our last days Stateside at Aunt Gertrude's house near Seattle. Now one could not pass through that home casually. It demanded considerable commitment. Our Rowland cousins lived elegantly, at a level of civilization unusual in a family with four young children. Mum and Auntie Norma doubtless had good cause for anxiety about the behavior of their four offspring in this unusual setting.

Surely the Youngberg children, nurtured in the jungles of the Tatau River in Sarawak, were ill equipped to cope with such refinement. Indeed, I'd assumed from the stories Madge told that out there they ate their meals daily either with the headhunters or in the society of crocodiles on the river bank. I know that I had never seen such a table setting in my life, not even in a book. White damask tablecloth, stemware and translucent china, and napkins the size of pillowcases! Moreover, the children's table in the kitchen pretty much duplicated the decor of the adults' in the dining room.

Our mothers hovered over us as we climbed into our chairs. "Now don't spill anything on Aunt Gertrude's nice tablecloth." "Don't break the glasses."

"Don't eat with your fingers." "Don't chew with your mouth open." "Don't make any noise."

Consequently, Jimmy, Ben and I sat paralyzed by our surroundings and crushed with the load of strictures laid upon us. We almost forgot about food. Only twelve-year-old Madge could cope. "Don't worry, Mom." She took charge with consummate confidence. ' 'I'll see to them." I caught the slight emphasis she put into the word "them."

As soon as our mothers were out of earshot, she fixed relentless blue eyes upon the three of us. "Now if any one of you spills anything on the tablecloth bigger than the size of this spoon, I'll never play with you again as long as you live."

Stricken by the solemnity of this injunction, we studied the small teaspoon and trembled. Not playing with Madge was a fate far too terrible to be comprehended. Was there no hope?

Madge laid the spoon down with deliberation. "But," she went on," if someone does spill something, he can be forgiven only if he eats twelve ants." We sighed with relief. Then one might transgress and still live! Of course, we agreed to the conditions. It never occurred to us that there could be a third option.

The meal commenced solemnly, everyone intent upon his personal responsibilities. Then it happened. Jimmy overturned his whole goblet of milk! His stubby, six-year-old fingers fumbled just once, and over it went. Aghast, we watched the milk puddle ooze around his plate.

"Well." Madge surveyed us evenly. "You know what that means."

We knew.

After breakfast we all scampered out into the front yard to hunt for ants. We foraged under the bushes, combed through the flower beds, and dug under the roots of trees. But we couldn't find any ants. Somehow none of us had reckoned with this possibility.

Near tears, Jimmy approached his sister. "But, Madge," he whispered, "we can't find ... "

"Just keep looking," she intoned from her throne on the front steps.

We renewed our search, rigid with desperation. What if we never found any? At last, we overturned a rotten log down by the fence. There a whole colony of fat white termites lay inert in the moist black earth. With a shout of delight, Jimmy seized two or three and ran to the porch with Ben and me close at his heels. "Madge! Madge! Will these do?" He opened his grubby little fist for her to see. She inspected the loathsome creatures minutely. " Yes, Jimmy. These will be all right." She followed us back to the log. "Remember. It has to be twelve."

Like Druids practicing the most sacred rites of the oak tree, we squatted in a circle. Jimmy picked out twelve termites. In silent awe we watched as he ate them.

The whole ceremony passed reverently, without pain or regret. Nothing but happiness and gratitude! The sinner had paid his price, and the gates of paradise had swung open to him once again.

And so, a joyous little company of disciples, we trouped back across the lawn to the house, following Madge. Wonderful, all-powerful Madge who probably had the next phase of our training already planned for us!

# CHAPTER 11

# Shipboard Capers

I had never seen the ocean before we arrived in Seattle for our trans-Pacific crossing. Neither had Mum, for that matter.

I had a specific picture in my mind of what it would be like, of course, but reality left me quite speechless. The noise and bigness of everything at the wharf made me hang onto Mum's hand a little more securely than I would have otherwise done. Nothing in my world heretofore had prepared me for this immensity. I don't remember saying goodbye to anyone before we walked up the gangplank to board the S.S. *Grant.* I'm sure that Uncle Wilson and Aunt Gertrude Rowland came to see us off, but I can't be sure. Everything that mattered most to me at that moment was also on the ship—Dad and Mum, Auntie Norma, Jimmy and Ben, and of course Madge. I wasn't leaving anything behind. I had it all with me. For the first few days even memories of Grandpa, Grandma, and Chariton dimmed.

Nothing in Kansas City or Chariton had given me the least preview of what the floating city of that ship turned out to be. The polished wood paneling, the crystal chandeliers, the carpets in the lounges and ballrooms. And our cabin! It took me a couple of hours to comprehend the compactness, the tidiness, the made-to-order convenience. Even the simplest things mystified me—beds built-in to the walls and made up with blinding-white linen, wardrobes for our luggage, bathroom fixtures fitted snugly together like a picture puzzle. Water pressure in the bathtub strong enough to have propelled the whole ship, I believe. Beside my bed a porthole opened out of a tiny alcove. All the world went by me while I stood with shoulders wedged into that round window. A round window? How wonderful!

I loved the low rumble of the engines way down under my bed somewhere. A lullaby that I've never tired of hearing all my life. It took me at least two days at sea to learn the ocean. I spent hours on deck just looking at the water. It mesmerized me! First the brown water turned to green, and then to blue, and finally to rich indigo, always laced with foam in everlastingly changing patterns on the swells. The ship's bows cut grandly into the waves while the sea gulls sailed overhead. At the back, the propeller churned up a frantic heap of water, leaving an agitated trail behind as far as I could see, clear to the horizon.

For some reason none of us kids had the least twinge of seasickness, not for the whole four weeks of the journey. Our favorite sport was running on the deck when the seas got high. As the ship rose, we'd almost lift off into the air. When it fell, we became heavy as elephants and could hardly pick up our feet. We ran in the rhythm of the waves, doing a kind of sailor's ballet down the companionways. I suppose this elemental dance must have been the beginning of my lifelong fascination with the sea.

Although the other passengers didn't merit much attention, the crew did. The officers wore white uniforms, gold braid and brass buttons. Everyone else had white jackets and black pants. I couldn't stop looking at them. The cabin boy was a friendly young lad. A mere teenager, I think. He came in every morning to make the beds and tidy the cabin. A novelty! I'd never before seen anyone do work for us. I rather liked the idea.

We kids ate in the children's dining room, an hour earlier than our parents. By being very small and very quiet, I could go once a week or so to see what went on in the big people's dining room. More men in white jackets and a great number of fancy people. I noticed that all the waiters in white jackets and black pants (whatever age they were) got called "Boy." There seemed to be someone shouting "Boy" every minute of the day.

The Big People "dressed" for dinner. One woman, with crimpy red hair and enough necklaces on to halter a horse, sat at Mum's and Dad's table. Her dress hung on her like the lace curtains in Grandma's piano room. She'd purse up her thin red lips and talk about how she'd "been abroad seventeen times." A comment designed to keep us all in our places, I guess. Instead of glasses, she had one lens on a stick. When she looked at me, she put it up to her eye as if she were examining a nasty little insect. I didn't like her, and after a couple of times I didn't beg to go to the big dining room and stand between my parents' chairs where she could see me.

The children's dining room had plenty of interest of its own. We sat eight children to a round table, attended by Boys. At first mothers, fathers or maids brought the kids to the table, but after a day or two most of them stopped coming, even ours. That gave me a heady sense of independence. I'd never eaten by myself before. This absence of supervision, of course, put more responsibility on the Boys.

I was accustomed to one dish, one cup, a fork, spoon and knife. Nothing more. The table settings even in the kids dining room were confusing. In the adults' room, of course, they completely floored me. Three plates, three goblets, a dozen pieces of silverware and other unidentified objects—all for one person! No wonder they needed Boys to carry the food. There was no room left on the table to set the dishes down, especially after you got the name-signs, the flower arrangement and the fingerbowls on as well.

The little girl to my left was a tyrant. She had stylishly cut black hair and very black eyebrows that she wiggled to make important effects. She constantly yelled at the Boys for some service or another. She might almost have been the child of that weird woman who had been abroad seventeen times. Except that No. 17 just didn't seem to be the type who would ever have bothered herself with anything so troublesome as children.

One evening our Boy served me my mashed potatoes and oily brown gravy. "Thank you," I said.

"Do you want to have some tomatoes too," he asked.

"Yes, please." I almost felt as if I'd been abroad at least twice myself, making decisions like that, all alone!

Then my seatmate sniffed loudly. "Humph! What are you saying please and thank you to him for?" She leaned forward in her chair. "He's only a Boy, you know!"

"But," the Boy replied in self defense, "it's always very nice to say. . ."

Before he could finish the sentence, the little girl suddenly turned to me and threw up. A great quantity. She must have been eating all afternoon. The poor Boy had to clean up the mess, of course. Another Boy removed the child, in considerable disarray, to her cabin.

A great silence fell over the table. Even Madge had no explanation to offer. To me, however, it looked like a visitation from heaven. While the girl was in the very act of being rude, an angel smote her! Very impressive! When she came back to breakfast the next morning, she was much quieter.

In our own way, we complicated the lives of the Boys. In addition to all the deck games we provided for ourselves, Madge, Jimmy and I discovered a new sport in the cabin. The alcove where the porthole was measured about twenty inches square. By lying across the bed and hanging on to one another's feet, we formed a continuous human chain. We went over the bed, down the alcove space, under the bed and up. Moving our four bodies while still hanging on to one another's feet required a difficult snake-like movement that took considerable energy and skill. Naturally the bedclothes got tossed off in the first round. Usually we ended the game by a general jumping on the beds. When we'd leave, the faithful cabin boy would come in and remake the beds and put the room to rights again. Sometimes he had to do it for us three or more times a day. I hope that he got a generous tip at the end of the month.

We steered northwest from Seattle, missing the Hawaiian islands. Instead, we sailed past the Aleutian Islands in a bitter, cold wind. Everyone got excited seeing the thin white line on the horizon. We already had ice freezing on the deck, so I couldn't see the point of it all.

Yokohama, Japan, was our first official port of call, followed by Shanghai, China. We stayed in each place for several days. Perhaps it's because the Orient is now so thoroughly blended into my life that I can't remember the specifics of how it all began. One memorable event from each place, however, identified those cities forever in my imagination.

Missionaries in Yokohama met us and gave us as much sightseeing as time and money permitted. We all went to a restaurant in Kobe where the *piece de resistance* in the meal was a great oval plate piled high with noodles. Uncut, they measured a full yard in length. We kids had never seen such a thing before, nor such an opportunity for innovation. We sucked, slurped,

Dorothy and Dad stood on the steps, joining the crowd on the cold deck of the *S.S. Grant*, all trying to catch a glimpse of the almost-invisible Aleutian Islands.,

and guzzled them down one by one. Great sport! Preoccupied with conversation, our mothers didn't notice us at first. When they did, however, they fell upon the children's plates with knives and forks and cut everything up. For unknown reasons, my plate got overlooked, and I went on, very quietly, sucking the long noodles down. The older children all watched me with envy. Not often did I get an advantage over them.

Shanghai, among other things offered us a nighttime ferry-boat journey through the city. The benches were crowded, punctuated with the glow of cigarettes here and there. We were supposed to be enjoying the view of the lights and the skyline. We did until Ben shattered the calm with a scream. Someone had planted a cigarette butt right on the little fellow's leg.

Our month was almost up, so perhaps we were all ready for the arrival. Enough of exotic sights and the artificiality of ship living. Time now to cast anchor in our new home-place. No wonder the word "harbor" has come to mean security and safety. Everyone needs a destination. Even I could understand that much.

Singapore was it. We dropped anchor on Saturday morning, August 22, 1936. Dad and Mum couldn't have had a better day for beginning their new life. It was their eighth wedding anniversary.

# Part II

# Between
# Two Worlds

# Between Two Worlds

When people start talking about hometowns, I realize how rootless my life really could have been, if it weren't for the Orient Connection. Then I tell them that my hometown is Singapore. I don't say that just to be sensational, even though the announcement usually does arouse a little surprise. Or at least curiosity. I say it because it's true.

I arrived there an anonymous, shy little girl. I departed an "almost-adolescent." Although still shy, I did have a visible identity all my own.

Not only did I have to cross the usual bridge between childhood and the teens, I was also, in another sense, a "divided" kid. I had loyalties on both sides of the world that would follow me the rest of my life. Perhaps, not inappro-

The *S.S. Grant* stayed a week in Japan. The family posed in front of the ocean liner that was their home for a month.

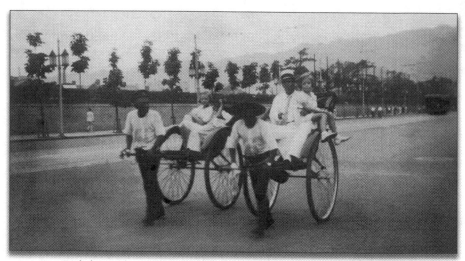

**Rickshaw riding in Yokohama, Japan (1936). Left: Madge and Jimmy.
Right: Gerald and Dorothy.**

priately, the two were linked by a third culture, the Far East. Whatever discrepancy might be discovered between my father's Australian roots and my mother's Mid-America background, somehow became easily resolved in my five years in Singapore. We all loved our new place and slipped into Oriental life with ease.

Almost from the start Dad began receiving respectful letters of application addressed to "Mr. Min Chin." Nearly everyone was startled to find, when they met him, that he wasn't Chinese. Perfectly at home, we had now become citizens of the world.

At the practical level, Singapore also offered Dad a way whereby he could finally climb out of the Depression. He could now manage a foothold in his profession and get on with a proper, life-sustaining career. Everything up to this point had been mere survival.

His sharp, inquiring mind had long ago committed Gerald Minchin to education. His love of travel told him that he didn't mind much where the appointment would be. When he was first offered an assignment as a missionary teacher, the invitation was to India. Whatever he went into, he did it with zeal. I can remember waking up in the middle of the night in our tiny

Kansas City bedroom to see Dad, with the light still on, sitting up in bed looking at books and talking to Mum about India.

After we'd been thinking India for several months, the locale changed to Singapore. Then Dad started a whole new cycle of intense study and anticipation. I didn't care. The main thing was that we were about to go somewhere. Never in my life have I ever tired of going! This single decision changed the direction of our lives forever.

# CHAPTER 12

# A Tropical Compound

A flat pancake of an island, Singapore fits like a tidy puzzle piece into the southern tip of the Malay Peninsula, south side of the Straits of Johore. Once nothing more than the fishing village in a swamp, old Temasek had already emerged as the "Cinderella of the Orient" by 1936. Sir Stamford Raffles, a shrewd employee of the East India Company, recognized its strategic location in 1819. He re-named it "Singapore" (City of the Lion) and claimed the settlement for the British Crown.

That morning, on August 22, a jaunty little pilot boat led our trans-Pacific ocean liner past the breakwater to a harbor mooring. Singapore had long basked in the honors of being the fifth busiest harbor in the world.

Collyer Quay was the face of Old Singapore, a city that has since been swallowed up by modern, high-rise buildings.

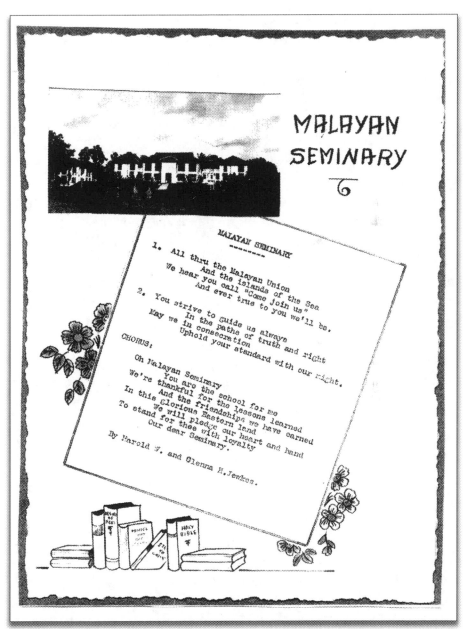

The Malayan Seminary on Upper Serangoon Road, Singapore, 1937. School spirit ran high with our own lively school song. After surviving World War II, the institution became Southeast Asia College.

Indeed, it rated as one of Britain's most prosperous colonial enterprises. Things looked good for all of us that day.

The foreign-mission workforce in this predominantly Chinese city was divided between two compounds. The Far Eastern Division administrators had just purchased an elegant old Mandarin mansion at 800 Thompson Road. It would become the office building, and the people over there would be getting new, custom-built houses, all in the best colonial style. The bungalows sat on high pillars, an arrangement which encouraged the circulation of air and amplified the slightest stir of a breeze. The luxury of air-conditioning was essentially unknown to us. Situated just one degree off the equator, Singapore never gave its inhabitants any reprieve from heat and humidity.

We, on the other hand, would live on the compound on Upper Serangoon Road, opposite the vast old city cemetery. We had three kinds of houses there. Two new ones of the sort to be built over on Thompson Road were occupied by the Len Bohners and the Allen Moons. Then came four middle-aged houses of a different style entirely. Appropriately they were also elevated four or five feet above the ground. We occupied one at the top of the hill, 10 Woodleigh Close. Below us were four lots where the old original wooden houses had once stood. Three had been demolished to make room for badminton and volleyball courts. The last house, empty and in its death-throes, still squatted on the fourth lot. It dated from the early 1920s when the Gus Youngbergs and the Wilson Rowlands had first come to Singapore in mission service.

The 300-student school, the Malayan Seminary, occupied the forefront of the compound. Life centered on an open quadrangle of classrooms and offices, with the second floor serving as the boys' dormitory. The kitchen and dining hall, faculty apartments and the girls' dormitory partially enclosed another square. By the front gate stood the printing press and the Union offices where Dad went to work every morning.

After the claustrophobic little rooms we had in Kansas City our middle aged Singapore house seemed palatial. Two slender royal palms flanked the walkway up to the little flight of stone steps with their neatly scrolled cement banisters. In fact, the formality was perhaps a little pompous for what was simply the door to a huge screened porch stretching across the entire front of the house. Inside, a long living-dining area ran down the right side while two bedrooms opened into the space on the left. Beyond the second bedroom was another small screened-in porch. Dad and Mum chose that for a bedroom. The screen wall opened to the outdoors. Their double bed almost filled the entire space. All the windows in the house had screens and wooden shutters but no glass.

Then came the house's "tail." A series of rooms on the left opened, one after another, onto a long, open passageway. The first concrete cell was our bathroom with a violent shower, an antique toilet with a high tank and long chain, and a little wash basin stuck onto the wall. We dispensed with such frivolities as a linen cupboard, counter-space, carpeting and curtains. Yet basically what more could one ask for? Indeed, the shower, albeit cold, rather impressed me. It had a lot more class than the suspended bucket with holes in the bottom that Dad put up in Kansas City.

This large bathroom offered certain unique opportunities.. Whenever we had little-girl visitors, I liked to soap the cement floor and turn the shower on full blast. Then we'd soap ourselves and cavort like seals on the rocks, squealing and pushing each other down the cool, slick runway.

We used the next room in the tail for ironing and for storage. The third room was the mysterious private kingdom of the servants, the *ayahs* (Malay) or *amahs* (Chinese). Down under the back steps the household help had three more little rooms—one for cooking their rice and one tiled for doing laundry. The third cubicle was their bathroom with a shower that beat right down onto their set-in-the-floor toilet. The latter mechanism fascinated me endlessly, and I hung around until our *ayah,* Mona, let me try it out one time.

I never lacked for children to play with on the compound, nor did we ever run out of entertainment. Few organized events were planned for us, and we had very few toys. Still, we had each other, and our world of imagination brimmed with fun and excitement.

Anyone just looking at us might have wondered what in the world we were doing. In the heat of the afternoon, for instance, we'd retreat into the cool, damp shadows of the retaining wall behind the press-and-office building.

Around that head-high wall, it always smelled moldy. An unlimited water source somewhere made the stones black with a velvet coat of moss perforated with tiny pale-green ferns. A fine private place to rest when we tired of rolling down the steep grassy banks in front of the school. We'd sit against the wall like a row of little Buddhas until we'd cooled off and decided what to do next.

The same high terrace provided us grand-stand seats for watching funerals. Our compound was situated opposite Singapore's main cemetery. First, there were military funerals with bands, smart uniforms, and coffins draped with the English Union Jack flag. Even now, I can never hear the "Dead March" from "Saul" without remembering what a great number of young soldiers in Singapore must have died in those years. At least one a week, and usually more.

The Chinese funerals also passed down Upper Serangoon Road, encumbered with the paper houses, umbrellas, and paper money to be burned at the cremation. Thus, these useful possessions, in the form of smoke, could accompany the spirit into the next world. The Hindus were a little more realistic. The uncovered corpse always lay in full view on its way to the burning place, garlanded with flowers and having two marigolds carefully laid on its eyes.

From that same vantage point we watched the more cheerful Kung Hee Fat Choy (Chinese New Year) celebrations. Particularly I liked the Dragon Parade, with acrobats, swinging lanterns and the great dragon himself, the center attraction. He writhed for half a block down the street, with a dozen men dancing under his yellow silk skin. He coyly played with his golden ball that an attendant always carried before him.

Failing either funerals or processions, however, I could still sit for hours just watching the city go by—hawkers with their portable restaurants balanced on their shoulder poles, beggars with scruffy babies, water carriers, bicycles and rumbling lorries (trucks), goats, water buffaloes and Brahmin cattle, rickshaws pulled by gaunt, hollow-chested men, and grass-cutters with their sickles hacking back the roadside grass. They worked oh-so-slowly, doing what was called the "government stroke."

Yet they needed to hurry. The constant hot weather and daily downpours of rain could cause even fence posts to sprout leaves. Grass and undergrowth grew with insane speed.

I especially loved the rain, often amid sunshine. It came on violently but usually didn't last long. At the first sound of rain pouring through the drain-pipes, I'd rip off my clothes, jump into my bathing suit and rush out into the garden. I could smell the greenness of the thick shrubs and the warm brown-ness of the earth. All the while the rain pounded down on my liberated little body like a waterfall. As if all the sluice gates in some celestial dam had opened up at once. We kids (for I wasn't the only one who kept the bathing suit ready for the sport) would sit in the storm drains that went dawn both sides of our street. In a matter of minutes, the water built up into a raging flood, channeled through the cement drains. It would take the last ounce of our strength to with-stand the on-rush of water and not be swept down to the bottom of the hill.

Then the fury would stop as suddenly as it had begun. The sun would spill over us, picking out every diamond-drop on the leaves and looking at its face in the clean water pools. When you've learned the true glories of rain and flood, you somehow can never be completely happy again living in a dry land that doesn't even know how to rain.

I always had a passionate fondness for animals. From babyhood I fellow-shipped with every dog and cat I met on the street. Not until my teen years, however, did I manage to keep pets on a permanent basis. We traveled too much, I suppose. Once a terribly emaciated, mangy dog crawled under our house and had two puppies. Immediately concerned, I spent hours under there

Within a few months of his arrival from Singapore, Gerald Minchin's responsibilities doubled. Left: The Signs Press and the offices of the Malayan Union shared this building (1936). As Education Secretary, he reported to work here. Right: He became principal of the Malayan Seminary, next door.

The Minchin house at 10 Woodleigh Close, on the compound on Upper Serangoon Road, Singapore. A simple colonial bungalow, it was a mansion compared to the family's previous living quarters in Kansas City.

caring for the family. Then somebody sent for the dogcatcher, and a wagon came and took the old mother away. I sadly watched her go, but some inner apprehension prevented my asking anyone what would happen to her next.

Officially I was allowed to keep the puppies under—not in—the house, of course. The bonding must have been poor, however, for they ran away when they were half-grown. Perhaps they ended up in a kitchen, for dog is a Chinese delicacy. Before that happened, however, Buddy Bohner, leader of the American boys on the compound, suggested an unusual use for the dogs. "Why don't we take them down to the Malay village and have some fun?" he suggested.

"And then what?" I couldn't see why we couldn't just play with the pups under the house the way we always did.

Buddy leaned forward confidentially. "They think dogs are dirty. If they touch one, they have to go to their church and do a whole lot of stuff to get clean again."

The idea sounded fascinating to me. So we each scooped up a puppy and ran down the hill to the Muslim settlement. We'd been there before, of course, but I doubt that we were ever the visitors the people were most eager to see. They eyed us in suspicious silence, especially when they saw the dogs.

"OK!" Buddy ran into a circle of children sitting under a travelers' palm tree. "Chase 'em."

Young pirates that we were, the two of us invaded the village single-handedly. We shoved the puppies onto everyone who couldn't get away from us in time. With all the scuffling and shouting on every side, we produced a very satisfying amount of turmoil. We touched everyone we could. Then, having polluted a large number of villagers and breathing hard from all the running, we lugged the puppies back home again.

We didn't leave the compound often. There were very few places to go and very few reasons for going even to the ones that did exist. Christmas and birthdays could mean a shopping trip to Change Alley, where, among the colorful stalls, a Singapore dollar or two could go a long way. Usually we went into Robinsons, the big English department store, only to look.

The coming and going of visitors meant visiting the ships, and Clifford Pier was a familiar and favorite resort. Especially if the ship were anchored out near the breakwater. That would mean we had to ride out in a launch and climb the rope stairway hung on the side of the ship. Whole herds of little *sampans* followed the passenger launches, full of skinny little brown boys. They waited for people to throw coins into the water, so that they could dive after them. Sometimes they stayed under so long I worried that they might have gone clear to the bottom of the harbor.

Saturday and Sunday meant church and picnics. While we usually went to the school chapel on our own compound, once in a while we'd go to the bigger church on Penang Road. Most of our overseas friends went there, so we always had a grand reunion of all the kids. Otherwise I didn't see much of them during the week. Therefore, we sometimes got a little carried away with our jubilation. Subjected to stern admonitions, the older children swung their legs tediously from the hard mahogany pews. The younger ones periodically had to be removed for corporal punishment. That usually took place out beside the stone-buttressed bank behind the church, a place known, conveniently, as the "Wailing Wall."

The Royal Botanical Gardens provided the only spot we had for picnicking, but they were so beautiful that no one minded that there wasn't any other place to go. The huge, spreading trees that shaded exotic shrubs seemed to live for no other purpose than having children climbing in them. Upon returning to Singapore after an absence of thirty years, I could still find the very tree and the very place where I'd spent so many lazy hours, draped over the smooth trunk like a sloth, full of egg sandwiches and bananas, dreaming big dreams.

A great tribe of monkeys pretty well ran the park. Mothers and babies, teenagers and scarred old warriors. They reared their families in perfect tranquility completely unafraid of people. I never found it possible to eat anything without giving the monkeys a matching bite at the same time. Should they find the park visitors ungenerous, however, they'd take care of their needs in their own way. The first time we took our car into the Gardens we had a problem. One monkey, having seen our lunch through the window, tore a hole in the rubbery roof of the Essex. He reached his long arm inside and tore bananas off the bunch lying on the top of the food basket.

At this distance in time, I marvel at how simple our lives were. How little we depended on either other people or material things for our good times. We seemed to have limitless resources, and what one kid couldn't think of the next one did. We lived, I believe, beyond the world of money. I'm astonished to think of how old I was before money really mattered in my life.

In this matter, I believe that I was very fortunate. I could always look to my future self as simply me. I could live here or there. I could make a living this way or that. I might or might not have money. (Naturally I hoped I'd have enough.) In any case, I could be sure of always being myself. I wasn't ever going to have to struggle to be somebody else. I see it now as a very liberating way to start life.

Yet, we didn't live in The Golden Age altogether in those Singapore years. Perhaps the main thing that put us in touch with the other part of the world was the Swimming Club.

# CHAPTER 13

# The Swimming Club

One of the major corruptions of the 300-year-old colonial tradition has been arrogance. It was compounded of wealth, leisure time and the opportunity to surround oneself with large numbers of servants. The latter carried on in the mainstream of living, while their masters and mistresses could drift into a kind of fantasyland. Added to that was the general conviction that natives had to be, by and large, ignorant and dishonest. Any number of other derogatory epithets could be applied. This attitude bred airs of superiority and delusions of intelligence that could lead the colonizers to embarrassing and even destructive ends.

Missionaries, however, usually tried to temper their impulses to colonial snobbery by working very hard. The American work ethic prevailed strongly, I believe, on our Singapore compounds. Nearly all of the workers were American. The exceptions were Dad, the Eric Johansons (from Australia) and the W. W. R. Lakes. An Anglo-Indian, Uncle Lake told of tiger hunts and intrigue in rajahs' palaces—information that remained the basis for my concept of India for half my life. Furthermore, any missionaries worth their salt would have an ingrained concern with service and a belief in brotherhood that also would spare them at least a few of the pitfalls inherent in the colonial situation.

Whatever the motivation, all the people I knew did work hard. In fact, we hadn't been more than six weeks in Singapore when Dad, in his job as Education Inspector, had to make an up-country trip to visit schools all through the Malay States and on into French Indo-China (Viet Nam), Cambodia, and Siam (Thailand).

Because my Dad prized his British heritage, he met and cultivated the friendship of sundry Englishmen around the colony. A rather amazing cross-section of society, actually. We had, also, a red-haired Irishman who ended up at our dinner table just about every time his ship was in port. The fact that he sailed on the *Queen Mary* lent him an aura that he could never have acquired by his own simple personality alone.

Even as kids today are enamored of space ships and intergalactic travel, we used to love the ships that floated thicker than seaweed in Singapore harbor, year round. We spent hours drawing ocean liners, correct in every detail, smoke blowing grandly from all of the funnels. Therefore, the significance of dining with a sailor off the *Queen Mary* could not be lost on me. I fancied him a high-ranking officer, though he was little more than a kid himself and must have been a very lowly functionary in the nautical hierarchy.

At the other end of the scale, we had Major Hardwick. Retired from military service, he'd settled himself on a prosperous rubber estate in Borneo and taken unto himself an Iban woman by whom he had three children. The Youngbergs had interested themselves in the family, and the eldest Hardwick daughter, June, had been sent to Singapore for school. She lived across the street with Uncle and Auntie Milne, and she and I become fast friends.

Whenever her father visited, he stayed in the Raffles Hotel downtown, but his visits out to our compound were never barren. He showed me his box of medals earned in World War I. Moreover, whatever gift he brought for June he brought another of the same for me. He supplied us with enough books to

**The Singapore Swimming Club was a weekly Minchin family ritual. There, for a couple of hours, they could escape the intense equatorial heat.**

stock a children's library. He knew his customers all right, for I read books both in and out of season. There was, in fact, only one thing that could really divert my attention from reading, and that was the Swimming Club.

Its 200 square miles completely surrounded by water, Singapore island didn't lack beaches. They were not, however, clean and white, nor was the surf particularly impressive. Besides, the murky water concealed poisonous fish, like the *ikan sembilan* that, with a single stab, could kill a person. Or failing that, the jellyfish would congregate in sluggish schools to vex swimmers. Moreover, the mundane life of fishermen in their villages still occupied much of the shoreline, and we had no real resorts.

All things considered, the Swimming Club became a useful, if prejudicial, enterprise. In fact, I can't remember hearing of another swimming pool in the whole city. At seven years old, I didn't see anything remarkable in the fact that the Club was open to white people only. Even if someone had explained the matter to me fully, I probably still couldn't have grasped all the implications. The fact that I was the only white kid attending the Malayan Seminary was something that I never really noticed until we moved to Australia. There I came upon great numbers of children who looked just like me. During the Singapore years, however, I had absolutely no consciousness of racial differences. No one mentioned the matter, so how would I know?

All I knew was that the Swimming Club had a marvelous big blue swimming pool with a tower of diving boards at one end and a carefully graduated children's pool at the other. Just below the tower lay the beach. A protective fence surrounded a sea pool, and no sharks or barracuda could get in. People wishing to swim with the jellyfish (which the fence did not exclude) and not minding getting seaweed tangled in their hair, were welcome to do so.

The dressing rooms at the Club had several subdivisions under "Gentlemen" and "Ladies," two being for boys and girls under twelve years attended by *amahs* and *ayahs*. A servant would be expected, of course, to rescue a drowning infant, in case of crisis. Even then, only the hands should be immersed in the water, nothing more. Tables with umbrellas surrounded the pool, and upstairs in the club house, there was a ball room, a library, and I don't know what else.

To join the club, you had to be recommended by a member. This would not only insure whiteness, but it also screened out people of any other undesirable qualities. Dad secured membership for us through a rather impressive personage who was the chief health officer for the Straits Settlements, as Singapore was then called. I don't know where Dad first met him, but I do remember riding in his car—something that put him in a class by himself, as far as I was concerned.

One day that very proper Englishman took us past the leper hospital, telling Dad and Mum the while about the work he did there. My knowledge of leprosy was almost entirely Bible-based, and my imagination supplied more than enough imagery, wherever the tragic tales themselves lacked specific detail.

"The incubation period can be up to fourteen years," I heard the doctor tell Dad as we were riding in his car one day. From the rest of the conversation I deduced that "incubation" meant how long it took to get sick after the bugs got into you. The heat notwithstanding, I rolled up the car window, hoping that the leprosy germs couldn't get in through the glass. It worried me for quite a long time. I might get leprosy, then, about the time I'd want to be starting college! Threats like this, however, never do get explained to children. Adults usually go on assuming that the kids didn't even hear the conversation.

The doctor's enabling Dad to join the Swimming Club happily opened up a whole new world of adventure for me. I forgot all about leprosy. Now, without fail on Tuesday afternoons our family went to the Swimming Club—and sometimes on Thursdays too. This was, of course, not work—just pure recreation.

A novel concept, I believe, among the missionaries because no one had ever done such a thing before. If some of the neighbors did question the propriety of this kind of carrying-on, all objections were soon swept away. First, Dad recommended the Len Bohners to become members, and that started the chain reaction until just about everyone on both compounds had joined. This meant that swimming time became a major social event for all of us. Hardly ever did we find ourselves at the club without some friends there too.

Yet, the fundamental bliss of the Swimming Club would have survived for me if there hadn't been another soul in the water except myself. Because we literally sweat all week, day and night, and the effect of being totally submerged in cool water was euphoric. I can't remember anyone teaching me to swim. Seemingly it was just something that everyone did automatically, I supposed.

I believe that removing me from the water would have been virtually impossible, except for one thing. We always ended the afternoon eating chips (French fries) drowned in tomato sauce (ketchup), at five cents a plate. Oh, yes, we ate other things too, but I can't remember what they were. Perhaps it was because the chips were so different from what we ate all the rest of the week. At home we pretty well lived off the land with Chinese curry, rice, *mee goring* (noodles) cucumbers and tropical fruit salad just about every day.

In season Mum used to enjoy durian in the back yard with some of the college students. Dad and I never became converts to the spiky green fruit, and we wouldn't tolerate it in the house. It smelled like a putrid blend of rotten onions and dirty socks, intensely acrid—like a country outhouse. I liked the tropical diet well enough, so I could never see why with all the good food available, anyone would want to persecute himself trying to eat durian. In contrast, some basic folk memory within me reached out for those potato chips by the swimming pool every week. How I loved them!

Mum could extract me from the water only with the promise of chips. Then, clean and damp with my straight wet hair pasted behind my ears, I'd go up to the Reading Room to tell Dad we were ready to eat. He always got out of the pool early enough to have at least half an hour with the latest newspapers and magazines.

I had to go through the Ball Room to reach him. Upstairs people ate teacakes off silver platters, and waiters with white towels folded over their arms served tea out of silver pots. I wondered why, if the towels were carried for cleaning up messes, they always looked so fresh and clean. Uneasily I wondered if those fancy people never made messes. Downstairs at the umbrella tables where we kids did spill stuff on ourselves and the patio floor, the waiters never seemed to have anything handy for clean-ups. Didn't make much sense!

On the way to the Library, I'd listen to the waltz music and watch the couples swaying among the potted palms while the high ceiling fans stirred the sea-breezes through the ballroom. The ladies in their long slim gowns looked like the faraway princesses in the books of fairy tales that Mr. Hardwick had given me.

So, with the music swinging in my head and my feet, I'd indulge myself in a dream or two. The men didn't interest me much, but the beautiful women in their arms seemed something to consider seriously. As they waltzed by, the perfumed breeze fluttered over me and stirred something so fragile, so delicate that I could hardly identify it as reality. It was, in fact, the faintest hint of desire, perhaps, indeed, the promise of womanhood itself.

So, intoxicated with loveliness, I'd float on into the reading room, as gracefully as my wooden clogs would permit. Seeing my Dad sitting there in the rattan-and-teak armchair reading always brought me back to earth. Then we'd go downstairs to eat chips by the swimming pool, I felt instinctively, the ladies upstairs never did that. The name "junk food" hadn't yet been invented, but even if it had, I doubt that I'd have paid any attention.

"Some day," I told myself, "I'll be beautiful like them, and I'll stop eating chips and tomato sauce." But, I thought to myself, not yet. Not quite yet.

# CHAPTER 14

# At My Desk

We hadn't been in Singapore many months when Dad faced a dramatic change in his work. Or, more correctly, an addition to his school inspection work. His crushing work load now made going to the Swimming Club an imperative for him.

It took years, however, for me to figure out the cause of all the commotion. At the time, the sudden changes completely baffled me. Our neighbor, the principal of the Malayan Seminary, was, almost overnight, sent back to America. Always plenty of ships in the harbor, so no great amount of time elapsed between the beginning of the problem and its solution.

No way could we kids figure it out. "Why are they leaving?" we asked, naturally enough. "Because Mr. B is sick." The adults would give us no other

Gerald Minchin's first car, a 1929 Essex. Dorothy was at least as proud as her father the day it came home.

answer, no matter how we tried to unravel the mystery.

"But when did he get sick?" I wanted to know. "I can't see that anything happened to him."

Dad and Buddy Bohner's father were standing out in front of our house looking at the new car Dad had just brought home, a 1929 Essex. Even the excitement of getting our car, however, dimmed in face of this sudden, impending disappearance of the school principal.

"He got sick while he was traveling up north," Dad said briefly. That didn't help much.

"But," I pestered, "he doesn't look sick to me."

"Well," Len Bohner winked at my Dad, "it's a disease people get from … ah … from using paper towels." I sensed that the men had effectively blocked me out of something that was private between them.

Once again, no one realized how much I needed an explanation, so it took a long time before I could use a paper towel without concern, wondering if I'd get a disease that would make people send me away. Fortunately, in those days, I didn't have a chance to see very many paper towels. For years, however, I would gladly use any towel (in whatever condition) rather than risk a paper towel.

Anyway, the paper-towel affair concluded with Dad's becoming school principal and keeping his school inspection work as well.

Meanwhile, the ten families on the two compounds had, together, enough children to start a little American school. This was not an unusual practice. After all, sticking by the American system and American textbooks would bypass some transition problems later on. So over on Thompson Road Mrs. Mildred Bradley kept a small school for this purpose.

I could … should … would … have been there, except for two things. First, with Dad thinking about going back to his home in Australia, it was by no means certain that I needed to be inducted into the American school system. Second, and more important, Dad felt that if he was the headmaster of the school then it ought to be good enough for his own child to attend. Any other arrangement would, somehow, cast a shadow on his endeavor.

Therefore, I started school … again. Actually, I was already a veteran student, having been in the classroom from babyhood. Entering Primary I in Singapore, however, constituted the official beginning of my academic life. For the next five years my teachers would be Chinese, some men and some women. My friends would be a great assortment of Chinese, Indian and Malay children. I don't believe I missed the American kids very much.

Of course, I did see them at the Swimming Club. Probably what made my supposed "isolation" so negligible, however, was the fact that the Americans near my age were all boys. By some unkind act of fate, the families who had daughters had had them way too soon. Older and away at the American high school in Shanghai, China (Far Eastern Academy), they came home a couple of times a year. Just long enough for me to admire, worship and be curious. Still, I never had enough time to know them very well—Betty and Naomi Bowers, Carol Campbell, and Beth Armstrong. They were patient with me, but to me they were like manikins in the windows of my life, somewhat akin to the beautiful ladies who danced at the Swimming Club. The Johansons and Hendershots didn't live on either compound but in Chinese houses in between. Their daughters, Bobbie Mae and Joyce, were near enough my age to have been comforting to me, but we didn't see each other very often. The same applied to Colleen Campbell far away over on Thompson Road.

**Dorothy enjoyed her Singapore girlfriends. One day a few of them lined up on the running board of Len Bohner's touring (convertible) car. From left: Tiorma Sibadogial (Borneo), Eileen, Dorothy, Ah Ching Tan (Singapore), and Eunice Tremenheere (Borneo).**

Other diversions for the kids included sitting on the embankment above Serangoon Road and seeing funerals go into the large, park-like Bidadari Cemetery across the street. At Chinese New Year, from the same location, they could watch the Dragon Dancers pass by.

They entertained themselves with a make-believe wedding (November 3, 1939). Front, from left: Eileen (flower girl), Stella Phang (bridegroom, in hat), Irene Wong (bride. Back, from left: _____, Dorothy Minchin (preacher, in hat), Maurine Tan and Bernice Lee (attendants).

The "Big Girls" of the Malayan Seminary deserved the admiration we little kids gave them (1939).

Having to play with boys posed special difficulties and only a few rewards. Every little girl needs some other little girls for friends. I shared my soul-secrets with Tiorma Sibadogiel (from Sumatra), June Hardwick and Eunice Tremenheere (from Borneo), Iris McCall and Visiyama Moses (of Indian descent), and three special Chinese girls, Bernice Lee, Maureen Tan, and Ah Ching (the daughter of Milnes' *amah*).

Together, the eight of us moved through the grades—Primary 2 followed by Standards 1, 2, and 3. Year by year, we sat together in the old-fashioned double desks in various combinations, always good friends. When I needed girls I had them—big girls for models, little girls for confidants, and then the boys to keep me alert.

All of these social intrigues aside, I discovered quite early what school really was all about. The real moment of truth came on my eighth birthday. In the tropics, even soon after the sunrise, you wake up with the clammy feeling that the day's already far spent. No doubt, that's why you immediately think that you're tired. When I awoke on that birthday morning, I had both youth and high spirits on my side.

I also had the house to myself at that impossibly early hour, as I wandered out onto the big screened verandah. I'm not sure what I expected. Perhaps I just got up on the general principle that one does not sleep in on one's birthday.

At the far right end of the porch stood the folding batik screen that Mum had made to give Dad some privacy at his desk. Many days of intense sunlight had streaked the rich browns and blacks in the folds, contrasting with the anemic faded lines of the exposed parts of the fabric. Bookshelves lined the screen inside, one inner wall and one outer. For my Dad browsing in bookstores was an almost religious exercise.

His desk stood against the fourth wall. Dad's most characteristic place in the entire house was his study. I knew better than to interrupt him at the typewriter or to remove his scissors from the desk drawer without his personal permission. Still, I liked to hang around, watching. Vaguely I wondered about the day when I would, as I used to say, "do big work like Daddy."

On this birthday morning, however, something on the verandah was definitely different. Some of the furniture had been moved out. When I discovered what the real difference was, I almost choked with excitement. At the far right end of the porch. directly opposite Dad's study on the left end, stood a little blond desk. Its matching chair turned out to be just the right size for my eight-year-old person. I sat down, dreamy as Goldilocks. Speechless with wonder, I looked at the card on the desk; "Happy Birthday, Dottie."

No mistaking for whom it was intended! Minutes passed in a trance-like glory before I could bring myself to touch the little black tray with its rainbow display of pencils, all trimmed to needle-sharp points. Inside the first drawer I found a fat pink eraser, a red ruler and a green pen-holder with half a dozen new nibs, plus a squat little bottle of Quink Ink. I saw my own scissors, put there for a purpose, I'm sure. Now Dad wouldn't always have to be hunting for his own. Then came several thick pieces of blotting paper to take care of the blunders I'd make. Since ballpoint pens hadn't yet been thought of, a growing child's several chores connected with writing included nibs to exchange, holders to clean, and those blotters to soak up the smudges. Plus ink to spill. It covered our hands, spotted our school uniforms, splattered the walls, and streaked our hair. It was all part of entering academia. Pencil writing back then was looked upon with extreme disfavor, almost as an insult to the teacher.

Another drawer held the paper, a neat little pile of scratch pads stacked in a pyramid. All that fresh, clean paper for me alone! I could print stories, practice the Palmer Method handwriting loops Grandpa Rhoads had taught me, or draw pictures of dogs and cows in spiky-grassed fields. Anything I wanted to do in the paper world! What adventure! All right there at my very own desk.

To work "like Daddy," my own adored Daddy, now had a whole new dimension. Perhaps that's why the challenge of a desk and virgin-new paper has remained until now one of the most powerful forces in my life.

The Music Students at the Malayan Seminary, Singapore (1938), were supervised by Mrs. Glenna Jewkes, seated (fifth from left) in the front. Dorothy and her little friends sat in front, at ground level. From left: Maurine Tan, Stella Phang, _____, Eunice Tremenheere, Dorothy Minchin, Bernice lee, Altje Macarewa, and Ah Ching Tan.

Did Dad ever know that that year's birthday gift would shape my whole career? A wise man he was, and, perhaps being a teacher, he knew that I would ultimately choose to walk the path he'd taken first. Still, I wish I'd told him so. He'd have been pleased to know how often that precious little desk blends into my big executive-size one today. He'd like to know, also, how very often I now seriously "do work like Daddy."

Concurrently with the Singapore sunrise that October day, I somehow felt my feet set upon the path of my life. The awareness drifted in upon me, however, more as a gentle, cloudy impression rather than a defined, understood message. It wouldn't materialize into a concrete goal, of course, until I went to college and chose my own career.

# CHAPTER 15

# A Baby Sister

I was eight years old when my sister Eileen was born. Deep into books and all kinds of imaginative enterprises, I'd pretty well adjusted to my only-child status. Not that I was averse to a baby sister. It's just that I didn't get much chance to work up enthusiasm for the event.

Shades of Queen Victoria still with us, nobody mentioned the matter to me at all. I even went with Mum on one of her visits to Dr. Elder. A pleasant old man, he looked like Santa Claus off duty and without a beard. It never occurred to me to wonder why Mum was seeing a doctor. Clueless as I was, I didn't notice anything different about her either. These affairs simply could not be discussed with a seven-year-old.

Therefore, Mum's announcement came upon me quite suddenly. I was rolling around on her bed under the fan one afternoon, and she was putting clothes in a little travel bag. Now that I noticed. Dad traveled a lot, but Mum? Where could she be going? The suitcase put me on immediate alert.

'I'm going to the hospital very soon now. I'll bring you home a baby brother or sister." She sat down on the edge of the bed as I bolted upright.

It took some time for the information to get processed in my head. "A baby? For us?" Somehow I'd never thought much about the possibility, though I knew that other people had babies. So here it was, and I had no idea how long it had been going on. "Well, what about me? What will I do?"

"Why you'll just stay here with Daddy. Then you can come to the hospital later and see the baby. Afterwards you can help us bring it home." Mum smiled, at ease.

But I felt shaken and insecure. "Then can I sleep with Daddy while you're gone? Please?"

"Of course." Mum snapped the little suitcase shut. "Then you can be company for him and take care of him for me."

That idea comforted me, but I still felt awash in a very large unknown ocean. How little I understood! "Does Daddy know that we're getting a baby?" I asked. Mum nodded. "How long has he known about it?" I really needed to know.

"For quite a long time, Dottie." Mum put her arm around me, and I felt a little better. But not much.

"Who else knows? When did Aunt Effie James find out?" I surmised that Mum's best friend over in the Division Office had been in on it. I realized that I'd missed a whole lot of something, but I wasn't quite sure what it was.

Baby sister Eileen arrived on September 13. She and Mum came home after ten days at the hospital—not because they were sick but because that's the way things were done in 1937.

I flung myself back on the bed and looked at the shiny green frangipani bush outside the screen wall. "Well, anyway, if you get another baby will you be sure to tell me about it right away? Next time I want to be first, OK?"

"Yes, right away," Mum promised. "But now let's get ready for this baby." Of course, I didn't know that for Dad and Mum getting babies wasn't an easy task. My own premature arrival had created havoc in the family. When I weighed in at four-and-a-half pounds, not only was my life in jeopardy, but Mum came very near death herself. So that time the doctor advised: "No more babies."

Pregnancy a few months after our arrival in Singapore must have been a rather terrifying prospect for them. Old Dr. Elder seemed unperturbed. "Having babies is perfectly normal," he insisted. "It's not a sickness."

Somehow his positive viewpoint made the whole thing turn out well. Therefore, Baby Eileen weighed in at eight pounds early one morning at the Sepoy Lines Hospital on Outram Road.

I don't think I'd ever been inside a hospital before. The long open outdoor corridors looked like the *amahs'* quarters at the back of our house, multiplied fifty times over. In fact we had two *amahs* now. Mum and Dad had taken the opportunity to let the poor old *ayah,* Mona, go. Too old and feeble, she couldn't be entrusted with the new baby. Now Ah Lin and Ah Chu occupied the back room. Ah Chu would do most of the housework and Ah Lin—young and alert—would do the cooking and care for the baby when Mum went back to teaching her Special English classes.

I'm not exactly sure what I expected in a baby sister. No one had discussed the matter with me, so I'd formulated my own opinions. Primarily I think I saw her as a useful ally on my side in the everlasting battles I fought with the boys on the compound. Sorely outnumbered, I'd been glad to hear that Mum had found us a girl instead of a boy at the hospital.

So I skipped cheerfully down the hall at Dad's side, heading for the maternity wards. We finally found Mum in one of the beds—looking about the same as usual, I thought. In her arms, however, lay something very small and all-over red. It was making a tremendous noise.

Somehow this wasn't exactly what I'd had in mind. I stood by the bed for quite a time and studied Eileen. I couldn't help being interested, of course. The tiny clenched fists and big toothless mouth really were rather extraordinary. But I couldn't see any immediate use for her. Who knows when I could take her out to play in the storm drains. How long until she could hold her own when we played "King of the Castle?" No, I couldn't look for much help here when I had to stand up to Buddy Bohner and the Wentland boys.

Suddenly, a big officious nursing sister bustled in. "All right. Feeding time. Everyone out." Her face looked almost as red as Eileen's. I couldn't understand why my being there got her so worked up. I hadn't done anyone any harm. "Out, I say."

I'd like to have stayed awhile to get used to the new idea, but almost before I could draw another breath, I was ejected from the room. I trudged across the lawn and sat down under the hibiscus hedge. Sadly I watched a large snail toil along the edge of the sidewalk, leaving his little trail of slime behind him. I envied him the simplicity of his life. He didn't have to worry about what to do with his baby sister.

Yesterday I'd been so excited when Daddy told me I had a baby sister. Now I just couldn't get all the pieces of the puzzle put together. Worst of all, I didn't know where I fitted in.

Temporarily, I could forget the problem because every night Dad let me jump on the bed and turn somersaults. We had a lot of high jinks, and I loved the rough-house. Moreover, Dad wasn't nearly as particular about bedtime as Mum was. He didn't care if I stayed up as late as he did, and I thought that was a neat arrangement.

Mum and Eileen spent ten days in the hospital, not because either one of them was sick but because at that time, women just couldn't have a baby, get up and walk off. Finally, at the end of their imprisonment, they came home. Daddy, Ah Lin and I had the crib all ready in the bedroom next to the sleeping-porch. All of that activity was good for me. At last I could begin to feel that I had some part in the event. I could help.

Since I'd never really played with dolls, I guess I lacked the fine touch for handling a baby. Yet, knowing that I needed the experience to help me belong, Mum let me hold Eileen the first day she came home. The red-faced nurse was far away, and I finally

**Dorothy and Eileen "playing nice" with the animal-and-doll family in the front yard**

began to feel kinship to the warm, soft little body that clung to my neck. In fact, I was beginning to swell blissfully with new love, responsibility and importance when the thing happened.

Eileen vomited on my shoulder. So much that it ran down my back! My reflexes being good, I promptly dropped her. Flat on the floor. Why hadn't anyone warned me that babies did disgusting things like that? Fortunately, only Ah Lin saw what happened. We picked her up, and she cried a little— but not more than usual. So no one else noticed. Fortunately, I wasn't very tall yet, so she hadn't had far to fall. I looked at her carefully. Nothing seemed to have cracked or broken off.

The next several months passed without incident. When, at last, Eileen could sit up in her high chair, she made a wonderfully entertaining addition at mealtimes. I liked the way she could throw food across the table and smear her milk through her hair.

Now I had begun to see some challenging possibilities in the special training I might give her. My first success was when she was about ten months old. I taught her how to climb out of her bed by herself. Heretofore Mum and Ah Lin could park her in her bed—a large crib—confident in the knowledge that she couldn't get away, no matter how loudly she protested her confinement.

I spent one whole afternoon's nap-time showing her how to do it. The operation was certainly not without risk to a small person whose head barely cleared the high railing. Still, I worked out an escape route which, after several trial runs, Eileen mastered. Her foxy blue eyes danced with excitement, and I felt well repaid for my efforts. I was glad to see her aptness as a pupil.

From that day forward Eileen accessed the entire house. Nothing was safe from her depredations, including my own private possessions. Still, I felt a new, satisfaction in having a baby sister. I could teach, and she could learn.

Some day, for sure, she'd help me fight the boys.

# CHAPTER 16

# My Battlefields

Before my sister Eileen's second birthday in 1939, World War II had begun. We soon began to hear about the "Battle of Britain." My British father, of course, was deeply concerned about the turn world events had taken.

The most memorable part Eileen and I had in those early war days, however, was our passionate love of the war songs. Not just the old stand-bys left over from World War I, like "It's a Long Way to Tipperary," and "Mademoiselle from Armentiers, Parlez-vous?" No. We liked the rip-snorting new songs from the music halls of London.

Dad brought home two or three records full of rhythm, sass and fight. The songs paralleled the daily news with titles like "We're Gonna Hang Out the Washing on the Siegfried Line... Have You Any Dirty Washing, Mother Dear." Another one went: "Hitler, remember Kaiser Bill! Hitler, you'd better make your will!" Little Eileen had a sharp ear for music and used to sit on her potty cheerfully belting out "Nasty Uncle Adolph."

We played the records incessantly, memorizing every word. Alternatively we listened to our nursery rhyme records, but either way, the songs had relatively the same effect upon us. After all, when you analyze the horror of twenty-four blackbirds baked in a pie, the tragic demise of Humpty Dumpty, or the tribulations of the Ten Little Indians, you have to admit that the children's songs are none too gentle either. One way and another, we learned early on that life's essentially a battlefield.

From infancy, however, I'd been taught the beauty and efficacy of saying prayers. Praying, I understood, was supposed to help. By this time, my bedtime prayers had become focused on three rather specific needs. They were so intensely private that I would never dream of praying about them in the presence of my parents or anyone else.

First, I worried about the war. Aware of the gnawing anxiety it had brought into our lives, I hit upon a very simple solution to the problem. If only God would see it my way and co-operate. I started praying nightly, in all good faith, that Adolph Hitler would die before morning. What joy if, come sunrise, they'd just find him cold dead in his bed. Then the war could end, and we wouldn't have any more bother. A good, practical idea! That prayer was, I believe, my main contribution to the war effort. After about two years, however, I had matured enough to realize that the world wasn't all that simple and that Hitler's departure would still leave a lot of trouble behind. So I ultimately gave up on that project.

For about the same period of time, I had another very personal request that I presented to the Almighty, several times a day. I wanted to have long, curly hair! Cousin Madge had braids, as did several other girls of my acquaintance. Length of hair had become the first thing I noticed about any female of whatever age. All the princesses in my Hardwick books, of course, had long flowing tresses, golden and wavy. What I actually possessed was very ordinary, coarse, dull-brown hair, bobbed very short. Straight as a plumb-line, it hadn't

Only after the move to Australia did Dorothy realize that she had been the only Caucasian kid in the Malayan Seminary, among 300 students. In a lineup in the school quadrangle, her blond head was matched—sort of—by a Sikh classmate wearing a turban.

the least suggestion of a bend in it, never mind curls. It was exceedingly thick, and Mum thinned it regularly, a measure which seemingly brought on a heavier crop next time round. Even what might have been an asset turned out to be a liability. All that mass of hair in the Singapore heat? With no air conditioning? Where we had to shower at least twice a day? Lop it off then. We can't cope with it all! In all honesty, I can now see her point, but I couldn't then.

So I prayed that one of two things would happen. First, that I would wake up in the morning, a miracle having occurred in the night. My hair would be long, falling in shimmering waves over the edge of the bed. I would then arise in a grace, tranquility and beauty so stunning that the whole family would fall back in astonishment at the wonder that had been visited upon us.

The alternative that I suggested to the Almighty was that He should cause Mum to have a vision, to understand the issue at stake, to undergo a change of heart, a conversion. One that would simply make her stop the barbering and permit the hair to grow. She cut Dad's hair all of the time, of course, but his situation was different. While hair cutting made him happy, the same operation (indeed, more or less the same style) made me wretched. There was no way Mum could have known my agony, for it was too keen a grief ever to be discussed openly.

Besides, I'm sure she never saw me when I took a handful of bobby-pins and went down to where the carpenters were working. I'd pick up the long curly wood shavings that fell from the plane and pin them to my head. Thus comforted I would toss my curls and confidently trot off to play with my Chinese friends. They rather liked the effect and always told me where carpenters were at work, The exercise brought me some degree of fulfillment. Instinctively, however, I knew better than to appear before Buddy and the Wentland boys in my wood-shaving curls.

Only the third one of my petitions was actually fulfilled while we lived in Singapore. A bicycle! True, Hitler did die eventually—but not before he'd caused a great deal of misery. (I still thought my first idea hadn't been a bad one.) Sadly, I had to turn fourteen before I entered into full command of my hair situation. I immediately let it grow with abandon, thick and flowing and, yes (with some help), curly!

The bicycle, however, did actually arrive for my tenth birthday, after I'd worked on the case for about two years. Having the unusual facility of a movable bar, it could be either a boy's or a girl's bike just with a simple adjustment. I raised or lowered the bar in accordance with how I happened to be getting on with Buddy and his friends at the moment. Perhaps if I'd been gifted with long wavy hair like the princesses in my books, I could have afforded to have been less of a tomboy.

While learning to ride the bike, I took several bad falls, of course. A couple of times I saw stars, literally—red and green ones. I had abrasions and bruises, some blood flowed and some welts came up. Not for a moment did I regret the bicycle. How could I? Not even when, many months later on my farewell ride, it required a blood sacrifice—the day before we left Singapore for Australia.

Even so, the physical conflicts were not necessarily the most frustrating of my trials. Flesh can heal, hair can grow, and dictators can fall. There exist still other, profoundly more difficult, problems. The long years of being an only child followed by other years of competition with the boys on the compound took their toll, I suppose. In any case, I had a lot of competition.

Buddy Bohner, with his parents, Len and Margaret Bohner, at Lake Toba, Sumatra. Buddy was the recognized "leader of the pack" among the children on the Singapore compound.

I actually enjoyed playing with Buddy and his friends. At times they even permitted me to play toy soldiers with them. That game was safer and less strenuous than trying to hold my own in "King of the Mountain." But, whatever they decided to do, I had to risk both body and soul to join with them in it. I think it was a classic love-hate relationship for all of us.

Buddy was my exclusive hero. The first time I'd seen him we were all at a party in Hendershots' house, a welcome for the newcomers, ourselves and the Bohners. Half a dozen of us kids spent the evening romping through the Chinese garden outside. From time to time, we made forays inside the house.

I don't remember precisely what Buddy's misdemeanor was, but, in the middle of festivities, his mother took him out of circulation and sat him down in a corner of the living room. She set him to copying music out of a hymnbook. A novel punishment that I'd never seen before. Buddy, apparently, had endured this discipline before. Because I was curious about how it worked, I hung around and watched him. After all, he was only a year older than I, so my strongest sympathies had been aroused.

"I only wish," he murmured gloomily, "that she'd just spank me and let me get on with other stuff." He sighed and drew another staff to fill in the notes. He seemed comforted that I stayed by him. But, good friends that we were, we still did a lot of fighting over the years.

I was only ten years old when Mum decided that I needed instruction concerning the birds, flowers and bees. I'd overheard her with one of her friends one day remarking that in the tropics girls "developed" earlier. Whatever that meant. So I can understand that she wanted to get the task accomplished before too late.

I, of course, had no means of discovering the facts of life unless my mother told me. Furthermore, the girls I played with didn't know any more than I did, because their mothers hadn't told them anything either. Most certainly no reading matter on the subject was available to us. Nor did the topic—perish the thought—ever come up in school. Therefore, when they did get down to it, mothers had little set speeches for their daughters, all about roses blooming and other lovely things.

I can't fault Mum on her instructions, although they did sound very peculiar and mightily inconvenient. She said, however, that I was supposed to be glad when this thing happened to me because then I would know that I was growing up. It was, in fact, a beautiful thing that God had planned. Then, we could have babies. And so on.

For all that she tried to emphasize the glory of it, I still fell to brooding darkly over the news. "Is it going to happen to Buddy Bohner too?" I asked suspiciously.

Startled, she stared at me. "Well ... er ... no. Boys don't ... "

'Then I don't see why I should have it, if he's going to get off free!" The magnitude of the inequality, the enormity of the injustice, came to me piece-meal, my frustration mounting.

"But, it's only girls." Mum tried to calm me. "Girls, you see, have this very special ... "

By now I'd worked up a real rage. It certainly ruined the beauty of the scene my mother had tried to create, but I didn't care.

So the boys thought they were gonna beat me again? Well, I'd fool them. Whenever that time came, I would have nothing to do with the thing. I'd simply walk off and leave it.

And I was supposed to be happy about it? Humbug! I'd show 'em.

# CHAPTER 17

# A Long Guest List

Dining out and sleeping out were two virtual unknowns in my life. In fact, I grew up only dimly aware that there were public places where you could do those things. I knew little about having to pay for those services because we always ate at home or in friends' houses.

Likewise, we slept at home or in friends' houses. Singapore did have a couple of fine old colonial hotels where important travelers went, and all kinds of people could be seen in the street cafes. Still, the real people that I knew almost never did these things. Consequently, all the years we lived in Singapore, we had a steady procession of visitors through our house.

It's natural that people living in a foreign country will want to spend at least a few social hours with other expatriates like themselves. It's one way of transplanting a bit of one's homeland to a faraway place. Together we observed birthdays, national holidays and, of course, Christmas, with considerable festivity. The friends and neighbors substituted for one another's families who were out of reach on the other side of the world.

I remember our fourth tropical Christmas better than our earlier ones. The ballroom in the Chinese mansion over on Thompson Road made an admirable place for celebration. What with the Depression and all, I think I'd never seen such an extravaganza before. Perhaps, in a sense, I never enjoyed a Christmas in quite the same way again.

I'm not sure where the tree came from, but it certainly didn't look Malaysian. And the presents! A heap as high as Eileen's head! The Japanese stores in those pre-World-War-II days bore little resemblance to the stereotypical Japanese commercial centers of today. Back then they were full of small, brilliantly colored bric-a-brac, lanterns, fans, porcelain birds and animals, flimsy toys on wheels, tin whistles and so forth—all very cheap.

Our Christmas crackers came all the way from England. Long "sausages" of colored paper, they contained all kinds of tiny trinkets. You pulled the two ends, and the canister detonated in a very satisfactory explosion, complete with a whiff of gunpowder smell. Then all of the goodies fell into your lap. So Christmas for us kids turned out to be a smorgasbord of many things, all of which delighted us with color and noise.

That year, 1939, Dad played Santa Claus. He must have been chosen for his wit and humor, certainly not for his build. He was rail-thin, and even after the pillow had been stuffed in the front he still looked lean. Since this was the first Christmas that Eileen would remember, Mum made sure that the toddler saw Dad put on the suit. Then, hopefully, she could enjoy the gift distribution later. So we both watched the attaching of the beard and the lacing of the boots. Amazing what one will do in the name of traditions! All these trimmings there on the equator had neither physical nor cultural connections, of course. Nonetheless, we all sang songs, ate American food and went as ethnic as the circumstances permitted.

My chief gift from Santa that year was a glamorous sea-green dresser set. If I still had it, it would be a prize antique. Tiny flowers had been hand painted on the back of the mirror, the brush and the comb. All the pieces fit into a decorative tray. Enchanted, I'd never before been entrusted with so grown-up a gift. As I think of it now, probably my parents hoped thereby to instill in me some interest in combing my hair and grooming.

While we middle-sized kids accepted Santa's performance with aplomb, the babies and toddlers had difficulty. Nothing in Singapore had conditioned them for the "Ho, Ho, Ho's" and the rakish cap dangling lopsidedly over the woolly beard. Even though she seemed to remember that her father was encased somewhere within the clownish outfit, poor Eileen whimpered and got a new stranglehold on Mum's neck. She'd have nothing to do with him. While some of the other babies screamed in a panic. the bigger girls chortled over their prizes and the boys road tested their Dinky Toy cars. Our mothers visited companionably with one another, the men told jokes. Over us all, Christmas music ground out at 78 rpms from the Victrola. This strange cacophony of sounds then blew out the windows, floated through bougainvillea bushes and the palm trees and spread across the city of Singapore.

Most missionaries will testify that the friendships formed overseas have a quality and intensity frequently missing from the more predictable relationships established at home. I thought of the men and women on the compounds, all of them, as uncles and aunts. I realize that they could have become so only because of the strong bond that must have existed between them and my parents. The people who've not left home would have trouble understanding how this kind of extended family can evolve.

The Minchin family at their rice-and-curry dinner (1938). Left to right: Dorothy, Eileen (in her high chair, feasting on cucumbers), Belle, Gerald.

Len Bohner rated high because he was Buddy's father and had the only other car on our compound besides Dad's. A gray convertible Essex touring car, the canvas roof went up and down with much noise and effort. Its yellow celluloid windows then had to be buttoned in. For us, however, the royal Daimlers at Buckingham Palace couldn't have been more impressive.

I loved the times we kids went joy riding in it in the cool of the evening. Because you couldn't drive that far on the island of Singapore, it was a big deal whenever we crossed over the causeway to Johore. I'd heard that tigers could swim the Straits, so I always hung over the side of the car hoping to glimpse one in transit.

We saw a lot of Harold and Glenna Jewkes. Their little girl, Elaine, was near Eileen's age. More than once the youngsters escaped their *amahs* at bath time and streaked between our two houses, naked as tadpoles. Then opposite us we had Uncle and Auntie Milne's house. Rather like the Youngbergs' home, it was always full of children.

As a single character, Mr. Hendershot was one of my favorites, along with Uncle Lake. He became so simply because every time he came to our house, he always noticed me. Seven-year- old me who had few claims to fame! An inspiring presence, at least 6' 2" tall and of noble girth, he filled any room he walked into with a grandeur. His black hair and genial face, his rumbling chuckles and explosions of laughter. Already I had enough of Eve in me to realize that Mr. Hendershot was a good-looking man—indeed, a handsome one. Moreover, I accounted him not just a friend of my parents but of me also, the thirty-five-year age difference notwithstanding.

That's why when Eileen stood on the front porch one day and announced, "Here comes Hendershot," I couldn't understand why Mum objected. I relayed the message back through to the kitchen. "Mum, Hendershot's coming."

My mother reproved me roundly as she hurried to the door. "You must call him Mr. Hendershot." Considering that everyone else just said "Hendershot," I thought the restriction very unfair.

One day he came over after a three-month itinerary in upper Malaysia. He'd been gone long enough to grow a fierce, thick black moustache that completely transformed his appearance. "Oh you're so handsome" someone tittered."

Someone else, a little more conservative, said, "It really doesn't look very natural, though."

The conversation flowed around and over my head. I looked at the great man who was the center of attention. "Well, I think ... " Silence fell as I began my pronouncement. "I think

From left, Pioneer missionary Captain G.F. Jones ("Little Jonesy"), his wife, Marion, and Tommy Cowen. A racetrack jockey before he became a Seventh-day Adventist, Mr. Cowen was a professional exterminator. He did well in the Far East where termites and cockroaches grew to a monstrous size.

that you can't be handsome and natural at the same time." I comprehended the implications of my statement only vaguely, but in view of the chatter going back and forth, I thought my remark sounded as profound as anything else that was being said. Naturally, because I liked him, I wanted to say something.

Briefly the silence deepened, and I felt every eye fixed on my small person. Mr. Hendershot laughed lightly, and the crowd roared. When my mother removed me out of the company, our little session in the bedroom depressed me. I'd only tried to be pleasant. How should I know that I'd insulted him? I guess I should have just called him "Hendershot" one more time and let it go at that.

Most memorable, I think, were the out-of-town visitors, a great variety of them. They came often, and sometimes stayed quite a long time. The front bedroom with its double bed was officially mine, but when visitors came it was the guest room.

Whenever I got to occupy the room, I spread my stuffed animals across the bed, usually having only a few inches left for myself. I always put the dog or teddy bear I liked best right next to me, arranging the others in a descending order of regard. The ones I liked least lay on the outer edge. Sometimes it took more than an hour and many turnings on of the light to re-arrange the order, so that no one would feel bad. What else could you do when you remembered that the chocolate teddy had slept close in for a week while the rabbit in the orange-striped pajamas had been out almost to the edge for a month? Or the blue dog had been exiled and even fallen off of the bed altogether for more than two months. All of this while the yellow monkey had had an inside berth for at least six weeks? A lot of worry for a young kid. Perhaps it was as well that I didn't sleep in the bed very often, or I'd never have had enough rest.

When guests came, I gathered up my animals in a heap and slept on the coconut floor matting in the living room. Not that I minded! I supposed sleeping on the floor to be perfectly normal and would often choose it even when I didn't have to. Could I take an estimate of our five years in Singapore, I suppose I was excluded from my room more than 50% of the time.

Tommy Cowen was an ex-jockey from Australia. A wiry little man with a grizzly gray beard and legs like inverted commas, he liked kids. At fairly regular intervals he traveled through the Orient exterminating white ants, cockroaches and other nameless pests. Mum and Dad were very glad to see him come after the white ants had drilled holes through a stack of Dad's precious books, and the silver fish had turned some of Mum's linen into a shabby kind of lace.

"Ah, well," Tommy would say, "I'll just knock up a little something for you." No question, his powders and evil smelling liquids did work.

One time my Uncle Gus Youngberg visited at the same time Tommy was with us. They had to share my bed. They both snored so loudly, that even from the living room I felt that I'd been awake all night. They snored a complicated duet with counterpoint, arpeggios and disharmony.

In the morning each blamed the other for ruining the night. I know they spoke the truth, but I decided my testimony would do no good, even though I believe I suffered more than anyone.

Very different, but equally interesting, were the Teasdales, also from Australia. A middle-aged couple, they arrived in the Orient. I never knew why they came, but they were "Health Food Specialists." As far as I knew we just ate food. Mum and Ah Lin knew how to cook, the rest of us knew how to eat, and we were all healthy.

Therefore I wondered why this seemingly simple sequence required experts. I guess there was a problem about cakes because of sugar, about the curry because of spices, and the bread because of its companion butter. As it turned out, my supreme favorite, the fried bananas dipped in powdered sugar that Ah Lin made, combined several culinary misdemeanors.

By and large though, we had to go on eating our way. Imported food was out of the question. Even some of the local products were beyond us. For example, the only fresh milk in the country was colossally expensive because it came from cows who lived in air-conditioned barns. That, I believe was the first time I found out about air-conditioning. How wonderful to think the sluggish, enervating Singapore heat that we had every day could be alleviated. In those days, however, only a few cows benefited from the luxury. It had nothing to do with us.

The chief inconvenience the Health Food Specialists gave us had to do with frequency of meals. Our family subscribed to the fairly unoriginal concept of eating three times a day. Mr. and Mrs. Teasdale, however, took turns explaining that we ought to eat only once a day. They did. When they pulled into their stalls at the table each noon-hour and loaded up, however, they heaped their plates high. Only with difficulty could they peer over the top. I liked seeing the vegetables roll down the rice-mountain. Because there was no rim left on the plate, the stuff just fell off onto the table.

Ships bound to and from Africa and India from the East all stopped in Singapore. The freight loading took all of a week, and any missionaries aboard would disembark to spend the time with us on our compound. That's how we discovered old Pastor Konigmacher. After fifty years in Africa he was being sent home, bereft of friends and family. He wanted to stay and die where he'd worked, but in their infinite wisdom the Church administration thought otherwise.

Confused and frustrated, he was brought out to our compound. Full of wonderful stories, he drew all of us kids to him magnetically. We could hardly give him peace to eat. He would scarcely speak to the adults, for they repre-

Music has been a prime activity in virtually every Minchin household in history. In Singapore, Gerald (director) and Leona Minchin (accompanist) founded the Men's Glee Club of the Malayan Seminary. Fascinated with their "Mosquito Song," Eileen greeted them as the "Zing-a-Wing Boys" when they came to our house for rehearsals.

sented the force which was dragging him back to America against his will. In fact, one day he was found boarding an Africa-bound ship he'd discovered in the harbor. He was removed "for his own good" and sent home as soon as possible. He died within weeks of his arrival, I later learned. A sad soul, but he left an indelible mark on us children.

Other kinds of excitement came out of Africa too. The Parsons family stayed at our house for a week. Age-wise, I fit in somewhere among their children, two boys and a girl. My general education and vision of the world expanded a great deal during the time they were there.

At first I introduced them to the fairly mild games which I played, My paper dolls, my "Authors Game," Tiddlywinks, Dominos, Parchesi and such. Buddy Bohner and Rankin and Roger Wentland even offered toy soldiers and a few rounds of "King of the Mountain." Then we tried "Ghosts" a rather stimulating night time sport which involved draping torn mosquito nets on the fence posts and then hiding in the darkest part of the garden and scaring ourselves silly. This game we'd learned from the very inventive Youngberg children.

Somehow this extensive menu of entertainment didn't impress the Parsons kids much, as I remember. Oddly enough I can't remember exactly what we did, although it was always loud and very physical. I recall just sitting much of the time and watching the uproar, rather like a teetotaler caught in a beer garden. I never knew that it was possible to do these things. To walk on top of the piano, to climb the drainpipes onto the roof, to stack the dining room chairs up to the ceiling and see who could knock a bottle of water off the top one. All of this— and much more—was too wonderful for me. I wanted to join in because it all looked like great fun, but I really didn't know how.

There remained, however, a still greater mystery. Repeatedly Mum or Dad would come in upon the battlefield and scold me! "Now, Dorothy! Stop this racket." "If you don't quit this row, you'll get the spanking of your life." "Get that tablecloth back on the table. No, you can't play mummies with it."

Now it had to be obvious to them that I was little more than a spectator at these orgies. Things were going on that I never in my wildest imagination would have thought a human body could encompass. These performances surpassed anything I'd read about in my book of Greek legends. Not even the tasks of Hercules could have demanded more endurance and physical prowess than the Parson Show. Yet I was the one who, symbolically, had to pay, in token, for all of the damages.

I sensed some vast, primeval injustice in the universe. I just couldn't understand it. Surely the people who committed the crimes ought to be the ones to suffer! Not until two decades later, with my own kids, would I come to a full understanding of the difficulty parents face in disciplining the children of other people. Back in those days, the experience caused me to struggle with a major theological issue. "Does virtue really pay after all?" I asked myself. The answer I got was "No."

At the same time, I couldn't help being invigorated by the Parsons' visit. Such exciting sport, to be sure, and I was sorry to see them go. Eventually the ship moved on, however, and the family departed. Later that same afternoon, I heard Dad sigh heavily as he told Mr. Bohner, "The only things we've got left standing upright in the house are the piano and the refrigerator."

We never had much money in our family, but our homes have always been rich in friends. Full of books, good conversation, music, and dogs, and sometimes birds, fish and cats too. We also had a lamb and later a monkey.

Given my choice today, I'd still choose that house, even with the piano overturned, rather than one so tidily perfect that a happy life cannot be lived in it.

# CHAPTER 18

# Borneo Blues

Our annual, one-month vacation in 1939 was a very special one. Uncle Gus and Auntie Norma Youngberg lived in Jesselton (now Kota Kinabalu) in British North Borneo. Mum, of course, wanted to visit her sister and family. As for me, my recollections of Cousins Madge, Jimmy and Ben remained lively and stimulating. I anticipated the journey with relish, especially since we'd be on the boat for three days.

We traveled on the ship *Vyner Brooke,* named for the current and the last of the White Rajahs of Sarawak. A small steamer, it easily negotiated the river into Kuching. (I still don't know why the founders gave the town the Malay name of "cat.") Sailing up the river past the celebrated Rajah's palace is my sole memory of Kuching. Five years later, however, there would be a grave in the Church of England cemetery there, and the name on the tombstone would be "Gustavus Benson Youngberg," dead at fifty-four years, a victim of the Japanese concentration camp. After that, Kuching would have a new meaning for us all.

Happily, all of that still lay hidden in the future, and Uncle Gus was still alive. He and his family were waiting for us to arrive at their mission station, perched high atop Signal Hill above Jesselton.

I enjoyed the *Vyner Brooke.* Although important on the run as a cargo ship, it still catered well to passengers. Elegantly, in fact. Afternoon tea was served daily with a dazzling display of sweet biscuits, cream cakes and chocolate eclairs, all free for the taking.

Also, I admired the officers, especially the lean, handsome Second Mate, resplendent in his white duck uniform and gold braid. He took me up on the bridge and let me steer the ship for one minute! Then he posed for a picture with the toddler Eileen wearing his officer's cap. The engineer (who called himself the "Chief Gingerbeer") was a stocky, round little man. Very jolly. He gave me a steamy, sweaty tour through the nether regions of the *Vyner Brooke*. These two engaging young Englishmen were unlike all of the other people I had ever known.

Next we stopped briefly in Brunei and went swimming on the beach while our ship loaded barrels of oil at Port Miri. We picked up some lovely, long, slim orange miter shells.

Finally we reached Jesselton. There the Youngberg house engulfed us, unlike any other house I'd ever seen. The rambling brown bungalow sat at the back of the property overlooking a little valley, with a rocky cliff to the left and the church and school buildings to the right.

Inside, the walls fairly bulged with children. Almost every time Uncle Gus made a jungle journey, he came back with at least one forlorn child. Someone sick who needed to see a doctor. Someone who ought to have a chance to go to school. Or someone who was just abandoned and needed love. Always room for one more. Beyond that, my uncle and aunt had compensated for their family's isolation of Signal Hill by filling their house with books.

Madge still controlled us all, firmly. Yet she never seemed to be manipulating us. She was an omnivorous reader. No, more than that. Books seemed to be a physical extension of her very body. Very catholic and unexpurgated, the breadth of her knowledge was incredible. I think I've never known a thirteen-year-old head so filled with amazing facts. I read books too, but I chiefly concerned myself with dragons and, of course, the princesses. Also the kind of book that Buddy Bohner had given me at my surprise eight-birthday party, *Legends of Animals Far and Near*. (I read that one three times, and still have it in my possession.)

Compared to what Madge read, all of this had to be mere trivia. She poured over medical textbooks, a precursor, perhaps, of her one day earning a PhD degree in nursing. At the time, however, she didn't envision any such a career. Instead, she planned to marry a Dutchman. "William of Orange was the most marvelous man who ever lived," she assured me. "I'm going to find a man just like him and marry him."

She had gleaned her information from a dog-eared blue book, Motley's

**Aboard the *Darval,* an inter-island ship between Singapore and Kuching, Sarawak. Left: Dorothy with an officer. Right: Eileen sat happily on the sidelines.**

*The Rise of the Dutch Republic.* I'd hardly seen the Bible handled with greater reverence. She underlined the most sacred passages. When a whole page was enlightening, she encircled the page number at the top. If it was very inspiring she circled it two or three times. If the revelation had been altogether soul-shattering, she marked the page in black crayon. Now Jimmy, Ben and I understood little of all this. In fact, I'd never even heard of William of Orange before.

One day, being weary of hearing Madge drool over him, I muttered, "Yeah. William of Orange Peelings."

I didn't say it loudly, but Madge heard the blasphemy and swung upon me in a steely rage. "Don't you ever say such a terrible thing again as long as you live. Don't even think it!" I wilted in her wrath. Her blue eyes fairly blazed. "I told you he was greatest man in the world? Why can't you listen?"

Neither Jimmy nor Ben appreciated the excellences of William of Orange any more than I did, but we all learned to keep our own counsel. Mainly we didn't like him because he alienated Madge's affections away from us.

With the house so full of people, Auntie Norma often let us fill up our tin plates with rice and curry and then eat wherever we pleased. Sometimes we climbed up on the rocks. Other times we sat in the flowerbeds over-looking the little trail down into the jungle. Or we'd take our dinners up into our Ship Tree.

Right by the front gate stood a low spreading tree with smooth gray branches. I don't know what kind it was, but it was admirably arranged for climbing. Tuned in as we all were to ocean travel, we easily transformed the tree into the ship.

Ben was the Captain because he was the smallest and could climb the highest, always with his pet baby monkey attached to the front of his shirt. (The monkey rode around with him all day, an accessory which Ben put on every morning, even before breakfast.) Jimmy served as the Chief Engineer. I was the Second Mate. Remembering my friend on the *Vyner Brooke*, however, I didn't mind that the monkey, being closer to the Captain, got to be First

Mate. We each had our own branches from which to carry out our duties. How we loved the breeze blowing up Signal Hill and the panoramic view of the China Sea far below us as we daily launched our imaginary vessel.

We'd play for hours in the tree, conscripting neighborhood children to sail with us as passengers. The client we most desired to serve, however, was Madge. It is quite plausible that she'd rather read than play boat with us. Still, her presence lent so much sophistication to any voyage that we seldom could take No for an answer.

One day, after we'd been particularly insistent, Madge unwillingly

Our powerful Cousin Madge Youngberg (standing) took charge of five of her devoted subjects. From left: Dorothy and Eileen, Eunice Tremenheere, Ben Youngberg, and June Hardwick.

consented to buy a ticket from us. Triumphantly, we led her out to the tree and showed her the best, most comfortable branch. 'This, Madam, is our most expensive, first-class cabin," we explained. "The purser will take care of your money. You just relax and enjoy reading. We'll attend to everything."

She arranged herself in the central fork of the tree, leaned back and opened *The Rise of the Dutch Republic.* Jimmy and I took up our posts of duty, Ben and the monkey shinnied up to the "bridge," and the voyage began.

Calm seas prevailed, and we sailed proudly away into the unknown. Then, suddenly, I heard water splashing. How could it be raining in such bright sunshine? We'd never had this kind of weather before!

Next, from the first class cabin issued a terrible scream of rage. Directly from the bridge overhead we saw a thin stream falling, pinpointing itself on the middle paragraph of page 157 of the *Dutch Republic.* Aghast, Jimmy, Ben and I looked on, helpless in the presence of such horror. Only the First Mate was relaxed. Very relaxed.

"Your rotten monkey, Ben!" Madge scrambled out of the tree holding the holy book to her heart. "Look what he's done!" She stalked back to the house. I almost thought she'd cry. "I'll never play with you again as long as I live," she threw back at us as she flung the screen door open and stomped inside.

Unrelieved silence fell upon our ship, heavy enough to have sunk the sturdiest vessel. What could anyone say? When, if ever, would Madge forgive us? It was enough to bankrupt even a large shipping company. What then of our small corporation? Of course, she did eventually pardon us. She had to, because we were such a wonderful audience.

Most of us kids slept on canvas cots out in the back screened porch. Madge provided bedtime stories nightly. Most of them were derived from history or medical books. She told the tales well, and I identified completely with them. After a couple of weeks I was tottering bundle of nerves, ravaged with every disease I'd heard about.

For instance, I had to look every morning to see if I had Green Mouth yet. It was apparently common and easily acquired in the tropics, a Technicolor complaint in which the inside of your mouth turned green and then peeled off in thick layers until your face was consumed. Then, at night I lay paralyzed, skin tingling and the sweat seeping into my sheet, sure that it was the onset of any one of a variety ulcers and leprosies, all of which ended in grotesque growths and amputations. My agonies and anxieties could have served a ninety-five-year-old hypochondriac.

Added to all of this were the ghost stories. Also interpretations of war pictures from the newspaper, freakish accidents, occult native Borneo folklore, news of malformed infants, and who knows what else. The repertoire was designed to keep the mind of an imaginative child in perpetual turmoil. But how we loved it all.

Madge could create the setting for her storytelling with consummate skill. More than once she led our little group of disciples down the forest trail, pointing out the proximities of the stars and reminding us of the madness brought on by the moon. When we got down deep among the trees, she imparted to us some of her most amazing information on snakes, tigers, wild boars, and poisonous man-eating plants.

One time she left us down there, suddenly abandoning us to the jungle. She darted back up the hill, but we couldn't keep up with her. We cried. We begged. We clung to one another in the dark, but to no avail in that Borneo night. Some of us stood rooted to the spot and wet our pants. Then the braver ones dragged us along, a huddled little band of a half-dozen tortured waifs with emotions completely spent.

Madge was already in bed when we staggered up onto the verandah. We could hardly wait for the next story to begin.

Meanwhile, my Dad had gone on a trek with Uncle Gus and the carriers, who all had the *bohongans* swinging rhythmically on their backs. Their trip involved looking at village schools, planning for church buildings, and pulling a lot of teeth. They'd been gone for several days, and Mum and Auntie Norma had been left to their sewing projects. There were always quantities of children needing clothes. The sisters visited a lot and looked after the kids, of course. In one sense, however, we pretty well looked after ourselves, totally captivated by Madge's stories.

That night, being still at a fever pitch after the jungle journey earlier in the evening, I succumbed to our last bedtime story. Although every part of the episode remains very clear in my mind, I shall, in all decency, spare the reader the grisly details of the narrative. It concerned a susceptible young medical student who went berserk over an unexpected encounter with parts of a cadaver out of the anatomy lab.

I lay on my cot, drenched in cold sweat, staring at the palm fronds brushing against the screen above my head. My circuits were all loaded. I was completely over-dosed. I tried to speak and couldn't make a sound, not even a croak. Then something within me snapped. Like the crazed medical student himself, I catapulted out of bed, shot through the door and down the hall. In a single leap, I hit Mum's bed, in the spot where Dad would have been if he'd been home. My mind completely gone, I sobbed hysterically. Wholly unable to explain what was wrong, I hung onto Mum in total panic.

Of course, Mum herself stiffened in alarm. Auntie Norma came in with a flashlight. The kids gravitated to the door to see the show. It took a while to get everything sorted out. Finally the uproar got traced back to Madge. I have no idea what happened to her that night. All I know is that I slept with Mum, fastened on to her more firmly than Ben's monkey ever clung to him.

The irony was that Madge—marvelous, brilliant Madge—had two totally opposing powers over us. First, we loved her for her stories and couldn't bear to miss them. She never failed to entertain us. When all else failed, she might lead us in a Hyena Party where we'd sit down in a row and howl non-stop for at least five minutes. I suspect that that activity did us some psychological good, draining off energy that might otherwise have been employed for nefarious purposes.

In responding to Madge's stories, however, we sank into such an emotional upheaval that we drove ourselves to the very edges of insanity. Aristotle the Greek is the one who advised us that fear and pity are mankind's most basic emotions. He pointed out that it's good to exercise them and keep them vigorous. Thereby, he said, we experience *katharsis* or cleansing. I don't know about the pity part, but I do know that when we embarked on the *Darval* to sail back to Singapore my capacity for fear was in great shape after a month of exercise and cleansing.

On a subsequent visit to Singapore, however, Madge reaped her reward.

One of the basic laws of life is that the crime often contains within itself its own punishment.

One evening our parents had left us alone for a few hours. The house, of course, was securely situated at the top of the compound's single street. Moreover, the *jaga* (watchman) down at the gate on Upper Serangoon Road could be counted on to screen out all intruders.

What no one could guard us against, however, were the fantasies of our own active imaginations. In the humid tropical night we children sat down on the front steps to watch the end-of-the-day rituals being enacted in the nearby houses. Directly across the street Auntie Milne was putting her many pet birds to bed on the front verandah.

Madge's exposition on a news item she'd seen in the morning paper, however, was far more engaging than the birds. A tiger had been brought down from up-country Malaya for shipment to a zoo somewhere. Unfortunately, he'd escaped before he reached the docks and was, even at that moment, loose in the city.

Now this was ripe stuff indeed. Jimmy and Ben sat wide-eyed while Madge, with some help from me, created the scenario. Despite the fact that Singapore then (as now) was a densely populated city, we knew that the tiger had come right down Serangoon Road to our compound. He had, of course, avoided the *jaga*. That meant that he'd turned in by the upper edge of the college campus and crept along the steep bank of long grass and brush that bordered our own yard.

Now, beginning to get really worried, we speculated as to why our parents had so carelessly abandoned us to such a ghastly end. Now we'd all be cut off in the innocence of youth. A pitiful loss to the world, to be sure.

Just then a breeze stirred the grasses, not more than twenty feet from where we sat huddled together in a clammy, sweaty little mass. Staring at the fence, we all saw him! His stripes shimmered darkly in the starlight. Some of us thought his eyes were shining yellow. Others argued green. In any case, we were all able to see that he was a very large, fierce animal.

The adrenalin flowed. Fear engulfed us like a tidal wave. Suddenly our fuses blew, all at once. Madge arose and, in a single leap, shot across the street to Milnes' house, the rest of us clinging to her skirt and crying convulsively. The fact that she was as scared as we were totally unnerved us.

In a pack we crashed through the door. The birds all woke up in a flurry of feathers and squawks. Blindly we lunged forward through the next door. We stampeded into the living room.

Understandably alarmed, the Milnes received us solicitously. Our eyes, literally bulging out of our heads, and our trembling little bodies bespoke absolute panic.

Uncle Milne went out to look. "There's no tiger out there," he said. We knew better. We couldn't help it if he couldn't see him!

Auntie brought us some cold drinks to cool our steamy fevered brains. Gratefully, we accepted the Milnes' invitation for all of us to stay in their house until our parents came home.

Although the tiger made news for the rest of the week, he was never found. Actually, being a prudent beast, he no doubt swam the Straits back to Johore. Then he would have returned to his jungle hideout, mystified no doubt, by the ways of the city.

We kids may well have been the only people in Singapore who ever saw him! Travelers may tell all the elephant-and-lion stories they wish from African safaris. Hunters in the north woods of America may speak of marauding bears. Big Foot may terrorize the Himalayas. But for us that night that tiger was more real than all other earthly terrors combined.

To be sure, a tiger in the mind is every bit as savage as one in the bush.

# CHAPTER 19

# Other Assorted Holidays

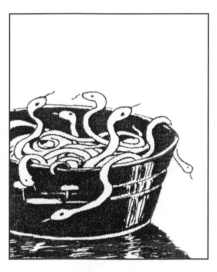

The unrelenting, equatorial heat of Singapore and the impossibility of our returning home to either America or Australia for furlough until after five years had a bright side. These circumstances earned us a full month's vacation in a cooler, more temperate climate every year.

Our first escape to the mountains took us to Sumatra. We shared the trip and a cottage with the Jewkes. For the first, and (almost) last time I sat on a pony, riding down the bridle path coura-

geously with Dad and Uncle Harold. Mum and Aunt Glenna almost never went out. Much later I figured out why. Both of them were pregnant, so that's why they lounged around the cottage gardens in the matching black silk pajamas they'd made for themselves. I still thought it odd to come on such a long trip and then waste their time in such a dull way.

The next year, when Eileen was about six weeks old, Dad packed up the Essex, and we headed north to the Cameron Highlands of central Malaya. There the cool, wet mountains heaved themselves up above the steamy jungled plains. I use the term "packed the Essex" advisedly, for our 1929 car had no trunk. That meant that all our supplies for a month had to be stacked on one side of the back seat. Eileen lay on a pillow between Mum and Dad in the front. I sat in the empty half of the back seat with Bit Moi, one of the college girls from Siam (Thailand). A capable Chinese teenager, she was going along to help with the housework and with the baby. (Mum was still not perfectly well since Eileen's coming.)

Naturally the car trip intrigued me, for I'd had very little experience in car travel. I turned out to be sturdier than Bit Moi. We left home in good form, with me showing her the collection of books I'd brought with me. The books calmed me, for I couldn't stay excited non-stop for the twelve-hour journey that lay ahead. Then I became deflated in a rather unexpected way.

We had just crossed the Straits into Johore Bahru when, without a sound or a word of warning, poor Bit Moi vomited all over me, the seat, the luggage and the back right car door, inside and out. Having never been carsick before, she probably didn't know it was coming and could not, therefore, be blamed. My situation, however, became considerably worse than when Eileen had thrown up all over me a couple of weeks earlier. Moreover, the Malaysian roads were not equipped with service stations or Triple-A quality restrooms.

The cleanup, therefore, was difficult and incomplete. The burden of the task fell on Dad while Eileen howled in Mum's arms in the front seat. I didn't cry, but I felt—with some justification—that I didn't deserve what I got. He re-arranged the cargo between us so that Bit-Moi and I each had a seat and a window. Although Dad tried, the damages to my dress, shoes and hair couldn't be repaired until we reached a river some hours later. There he helped me bathe in my dirty clothes. Not surprisingly, I felt rather sober for the rest of the journey.

Well after dark we left the lowlands and climbed thirty-seven miles up to the town of Tanah Rata. The

A picnic at Kota Tingii Falls in Johore was where you could really escape the Singapore heat. Dorothy remained obediently in the cold pool in the foreground while the adults frolicked in the waterfall itself.

primitive road wound through endless curves with the black, dripping jungle closing in on both sides. A perfect setting for seeing tigers, but none showed themselves. Also, Providence did not require that we should have a flat tire, though I can't help thinking that we'd earned one on that rough road.

Near midnight we stepped in out of the rain and on to the verandah of the bungalow we'd reserved. I'd completely forgotten what it was to feel cold, and I didn't particularly like the sensation. Sick as she was, Bit-Moi built a fire and heated water for us all to have baths. No question, we needed them!

By the next morning we all felt better, and we arose to a marvelous sunrise. Trails led us through banks of giant tree ferns, diamond-sparkled with dew. They stood knee-deep in tangled dark green vines, entwined with orchids. Then we watched the mists roll themselves up out of the blue valleys. When I stopped to examine an insect-trap plant, one of its big canister-shaped flowers dumped half a quart of water on me.

What really interested me, though, was the hope of seeing tigers. The caretaker assured us that there were plenty around, but all in vain. Bit-Moi supported Mum's injunctions about never walking out after dark, so my wish couldn't be fulfilled. With both of them watching me, I hadn't a chance for escape.

Missing the tigers notwithstanding, we had a fine holiday. The coolness, the wildflowers, having Dad home and available all day—all were novelties to me. Then the tea plantations demanded attention. We watched crews of Indian tea-pickers with baskets strapped to their heads, working the emerald-green hillsides. When we walked into the fields, the tea bushes, with their oak-hard branches, nearly tore our clothes off.

Another day we drove to the top of Gunong (mountain) Brinchang. From the peak we could see dark green lumps of jungle poking up through the clouds, like spinach floating in cream soup. Roadside vendors sold garlands of golden and brown everlasting flowers and displayed boxes of enormous, preserved butterflies. I never knew before how full of wonder the world could be.

The diversions, of course, had to end, and we finally re-wound our way back down onto the plains through the rubber plantations and the coconut groves.

Like Singapore, the island of Penang had been an East India Company Factory (trading center). I know now that it had many attractions, all the way from scenic beaches to the Temple of Paradise with its seven-storey pagoda.

Only one location, however, remains with me from those days, and that is burned into my soul, deep enough to last for both time and eternity. It's the Snake Temple. A hundred years earlier this Buddhist shrine had been dedicated to the Chinese monk, Chor Su Kong. When a large number of poisonous pit vipers had mysteriously appeared in it, people assumed that the snakes were the reincarnations of the holy man's disciples. Today the temple's been refined and organized, but back in 1937 the building was raw.

A long, shallow flight of steps (lined with beggars on both sides) approached the temple door. In the main room an island full of potted plants filled the center of the room. Vines crept up the dark walls and into the rafters. The place was alive with snakes, hanging, stretching, curling, sleeping. Heavy incense made it hard to breathe.

I hung onto Dad's hand and made myself as small as possible as I walked, in a daze, among the snake-infested plants. Eager to show us everything, the caretaker took us around the back where some very large snakes lay in cages. Then, in the middle of the passageway, leaving mere inches of space between itself and the potted plants, stood a large tin wash tub. In it were dozens of snakes that an attendant was stirring with a broomstick, like wet noodles in a pot. "We give them bath, *Tuan*." He gave us a genial, toothless grin.

How to get by the tub with the snakes slithering up over the edge, tongues darting and heads waving on all sides? Being left behind, however, was worse than passing the writhing snake stew. So I edged past, eyes straining out of my head as I focused on the tub. Just then, the strap of my *topee* (sun helmet) broke loose and fell across my neck. I knew, absolutely, that one of the snakes had dropped from the ceiling and had wrapped itself around me. With one single, piercing yell, I lunged past the tub and flung myself at Dad, clinging to his knees. Then came another shriek and another. I can still hear myself screaming.

The commotion, of course, took everyone by surprise. Embarrassed, Dad thrust me out of the sacred temple that I had defiled with my noise. I sat down on the steps among the beggars to finish my sniffling. It took at least fifteen minutes before I could stop shaking. After what I'd been through, I felt warm and much comforted to be out there with the beggars in the sunshine. Meanwhile, Eileen, too young to know where she was, could view the Snake Temple calmly from Mum's arms.

In May, 1940, we went to Java. By then I'd grown accustomed to the amenities of the hill-stations. Travel had become an expected way of life, and I got on and off boats as casually as most people walk in and out of their front door.

On that trip we stayed in a couple of Dutch hotels. We'd long

Recreating an American Christmas in equatorial Singapore took some sacrifice and ingenuity. The year Gerald played Santa, Eileen approached him very cautiously—although she had watched him put on the costume.

ago adopted some colonial Dutch comforts at home. Each member of our family, for instance, had a "Dutch Wife," a fat bolster about three feet long over which they draped themselves at night. Surprisingly, it alleviated the heat. Mum even made a tiny Dutch Wife for Baby Eileen. The Dutch afternoon teas also featured excellent baked goods of a quality I'd never seen anywhere else.

After a few days in Batavia (now Djakarta) we went up to Bandung, the hill station with the circle view of some of the loveliest landscape in the world. Little did anyone know that we were about to witness a way of life disappear.

On May 10, 1940, Germany invaded Holland. Repercussions in the Orient were immediate. Mum's and Dad's missionary friends in Java, most of them Germans, went into internment camp almost instantaneously. One day the friends were all enjoying a social evening together in Batavia, and the next day they were all gone. A couple of the men traveling on the train were arrested even before they could get home one more time.

Five days later Rotterdam was bombed, and the day after that, the Netherlands fell to the Nazis. Although I understood little, I knew something had gone terribly wrong—in just a matter of hours.

We returned home to Singapore. I suppose no one could realize then that an era was ending. Not only would the

**On her birthday, Eileen concentrated fiercely on getting all of the candles blown out.**

Dutch Empire itself disintegrate, but our British Empire would never be the same again.

For our family too, change would come. Dad and Mum now began talking about going to Australia. They would return to the Orient, of course, Or so they thought.

"When the time comes," Dad asked me one day while I stood watching him hammer out a letter on his little Remington typewriter, "How would you like to go to school in Australia?"

Would I like to go? Need he ask? I flopped down on the cot beside his sun-faded batik screen, eager to hear more. We talked about Avondale College, where he'd once gone to school. About his family in Australia that he hadn't seen for seventeen years. We talked about a great many things. For a brief half hour I glimpsed what it was going to be like when I grew up. The vision that day was very transitory, and neither of us could guess the deep rivers our family still had to cross. Anyway, at the end of our talk, he promised to buy me a typewriter when I went away to school.

How did he know that I would spend my life learning, teaching and loving the written word? Was he a prophet? Maybe.

# CHAPTER 20

# The Sell Out

In our fifth year in Singapore we couldn't plan for our annual vacation as we had in the first four years. This time our trip would be something much better, a whole year of furlough.

As befitted their trans-Pacific marriage, Dad and Mum planned six months in Australia and six in America. Plans can change, however, with lightning suddenness, especially with the shadows of World War II now hanging low over the Pacific.

To begin with, family plans changed even before we left Singapore. Dad was on itinerary in Sarawak at the time. The long succession of schools that must be visited had lengthened during his term of office. Along with that, he still grappled with financial problems, teacher-training concerns, and the administration of the Malayan Seminary. The pressure of years of overwork had mounted imperceptibly, and, finally, the inevitable occurred.

He was with our friends, the Lakes, in Kuching when he collapsed, a total nervous breakdown. A practical nurse, Lake and his wife cared for him until he was able to travel. Although he came home a sick man, he didn't seem so to Eileen and me. A three-year-old and an eleven-year-old simply don't have the capacity for recognizing exhaustion. Besides, parents have to be indestructible, don't they?

Fortunately, the mission administrators were wiser than we were. They permitted our family to leave on furlough three months early. Then Dad could rest and come back ready for another term of service in the Far East. Ironically, our leaving early was just the necessary amount of time needed for us to escape the Japanese invasion and the Fall of Singapore on February 15, 1942.

With some kind of uncanny insight, Dad and Mum decided that there were so many uncertainties that they ought to sell off everything and make the move to Australia a complete one. This decision meant they were virtually the last family to leave Singapore in an ordinary, domestic way. They sold the furniture and the car and took the money (such as it was) away with them. Our friends, on the other hand, would lose every thing they owned when they left. In the air raids on Singapore that began in January, 1942, some of them didn't even salvage the suitcases they were allowed to carry onto the refugee ship.

Although our auction sale was a sad time, it was at least a normal event. Our simple possessions suddenly were spread out irreverently in front of everyone. I didn't like it, but no one asked for my opinion. For the first time in their life together, Dad couldn't help much with the confusion, and Mum had to bear most of the burden of selling and packing. Still, I was so preoccupied with the forthcoming trip to Australia that much of what transpired in the house escaped me altogether. Already I had set my face toward another world.

My Dad had left Australia as a twenty-three-year-old bachelor and sailed for America. After a three-year-detour in Hawaii, he'd gone on to a college in midwestern America and married an Iowa girl. His younger brother, Len Minchin, had meanwhile

The Gerald H. Minchin family in Singapore, 1939

married May, a sweet, gentle nurse. He had settled into his pastoral duties in Sydney, and had started rearing a family of five children.

Now the time had come for the two families to meet. Dad longed intensely for the sunburnt land where he'd been born. Eager that their children should enjoy one another as much as they'd done as two boys back on the farm in Western Australia, our fathers set us to getting acquainted through letter-writing.

For some months I'd been receiving stiff, formal communications from Cousins Kelvin, Joan and Yvonne. They were written with rigid perfection, according to the regulations prescribed in Grades 4 and 6. Even the twins in Grade I wrote painstaking epistles. Those letters gave me hours of happy expectation. Moreover, we'd also exchanged pictures that we had studied like ambitious students cramming for an examination. We assiduously observed every button and shoelace, every bush and tree. These letters filled me with a passionate desire to go home to Australia. Dad had prepared me so thoroughly that I knew I'd be "going home" even though I'd never been there before.

Of course, I replied in kind. Never a good penman, however, I realized that my letters hardly matched theirs—the ones so carefully framed in wide margins, the large, round letters, spattered with erasures and sometimes tears. How hard we tried to impress one another!

Still, through all of the formalities, something wonderful had already begun to happen, the dawning of a great love and a bond of companionship that would endure unblemished for the rest of our lives.

With all of these expectations and dreams whirling through my mind, I took our last days in Singapore with little discomfort. All my family of stuffed animals were safely packed, along with the books, into the six sturdy wooden boxes that Grandpa Rhoads had built for us when we left America. What did I have to lose? I had it all. Poor Mum lost, though. She'd bought a beautiful set of English china, her first set of really good dishes. Then, a few weeks later in Perth, she had to stand transfixed on the dock in Fremantle watching the unloading of our freight. The crane dropped the box of dishes on the wharf, and they exploded like a bomb. Out of the whole set just one single eggcup survived. The rest became splinters.

Only one thing happened, however, to dim the glory of my departure from Singapore, "City of the Lion." It called for some fortitude on my part. The day before our ship sailed, I took my last ride down the hill on my beloved bicycle. It had been sold to my friend Maurine Tan for five dollars. I grieved much for its going, even though she was my friend. Nonetheless, I was eleven now, and I knew that I had to bear the loss.

At the bottom of the hill, I swung to the right to ride past the Malay village and on to Bohner's house. A skiff of gravel covered the rough cement of the road, however, and it threw me into a skid. I crashed down on my right knee. At first, I didn't feel the pain, but when I looked down, I saw that my whole kneecap had been torn open. The blood welled out of it like a scarlet lava flow, coursing thick and hot down my leg. I picked up the bicycle and started walking back up the hill, the blood squishing in my shoe.

Suddenly the pain hit, and I gasped for breath. I staggered on in blind shock, the unshed tears choking up in my throat. Some college boys were playing on the badminton court. One of them started up, alarmed. "Your leg!" he cried. "Let me help you!"

Recently, however, I'd become conscious of boys in a kind of new way. The feeling hit me occasionally, at odd times. So today I didn't want the boys to see me cry. "Oh, no. It's all right," I lied. "I'm fine."

By the time I reached the front door, however, all my strength—physical and emotional—had drained away. I hadn't cried yet. I stumbled into the house, unthinking, tracking blood across the coconut floor- matting. "Mum!" I screamed. "Mum! Oh, Oh! Mama … Mama," I wailed. "Help! Help me!" I couldn't hold out another minute.

Although she was in the shower, in seconds she burst out the door in her housecoat. "Dottie!" she cried, looking at the mess. "Whatever has happened?"

The moment I heard her voice, the floodgates opened. I broke into a torrent of hysterical crying and fell in a heap on the kitchen floor. Dad rushed in from the back yard. All right. I was home, in Mum's arms. I didn't have to pretend any more. She picked me up, stopped the bleeding, and held me while I cried myself to exhaustion.

So, I was still a very small girl, after all. I'm certain that the wound should have been stitched. That day, though, home treatment had to suffice. Tomorrow, Thursday, March 20, 1941, we would sail for Australia.

Today with the advent of air-travel we've lost something quite irretrievable. Ship departures used to have a sentimental, leisurely atmosphere. It can't be duplicated in a vast air terminal with thousands of harried passengers rushing through the concourse and with hijackers plotting terrorism. Everyone should have a chance to go away at least once on a ship. It's something that's done with such gentility.

First your family and friends come aboard to help you carry your luggage. They see your cabin where you'll be living for the next days or weeks. They wander all over the ship and see the parlors, dining rooms, swimming pools, libraries and so on. All the while the engines have been throbbing like a gentle heartbeat, somewhere far down below.

Then the cry goes up: "All ashore that's going ashore." You hug and kiss and cry and linger over the last messages. Finally, your friends go down the gangplank and leave you on the deck. Still, plenty of time, while the stevedores throw the great coils of rope off the anchor posts. The ship hasn't moved yet.

Now is the time for the streamers. You and the other people on deck have some and the crowd down below on the dock have some more. You toss these rainbow-colored rolls of paper to one another. Friends hold the streamers in pairs, trying to transmit their love through the paper lines. Hundreds of streamers tie the boat to the dock.

Then you look down and see the water-space between the ship and the pylons of the wharf widening. It is a slow, irresistible movement that you are powerless to stop. The streamers stretch taut and begin to break, one by one, each falling limp into the oily water. More tears and blown kisses. Soon we'll be out of earshot. Then the last streamer snaps. You stand at the railing holding your broken piece, and your friends stand below on the steadily diminishing wharf holding theirs.

You've said goodbye in slow motion. You're sensitive to every step of the process. You've had time to think and savor the moment, and you'll never forget it. Even a kid can understand what it means. It's a gift that an airport never gives you.

You watch for a long time, until the people on the wharf shrink into the shadowy outline of the harbor warehouses. Finally, you drop your broken streamer into the water and go inside.

A new chapter is beginning. You step over the high threshold, waltz down the great polished oak stairway and run along the narrow companionway to your cabin. En route you overhear some ladies wondering who'll be invited to sit at the captain's table this first night at dinner. You hope there's ice cream on the menu, and you remember how good it tastes, served in a heavy silver goblet and standing on a fancy paper doily.

The war in the Pacific hasn't started, yet.

# Part III

# The Australian Heritage

# PART III

# The Australian Heritage

In 1829 my Australian ancestors, the Minchins, emigrated from the town of Petersfield, Hampshire, England. Before that, a succession of younger sons, displaced in the landowning system, had sojourned for several decades in County Tipperary, Ireland. Many had scattered to the British colonies. Still earlier, back in the 15th century, the Minchins had been tenants of a manor in the Cotswolds in Gloucestershire. The Hitchcocks came from the pleasant village of Waddesdon, Buckinghamshire, arriving in the Australia in 1842.

Thus, in the mid-19th century the two families converged on John Peel's settlement on the Swan River, West Australia. The modem prosperity of the cities of Perth and Fremantle belies the stringency of those pioneer days when

**Sketch of Spring Park Farm (1876). Gerald's Grandfather Alfred Minchin homesteaded this land on the bank of the Swan River. The fronts of the buildings faced the river.**

**Left: Alfred and Lucy Martin-Minchin beside their mud-brick cottage (1900). Above: Granddaughter Jean Gardiner stands in the very barren kitchen in the pioneer home (1960).**

my great-great-grandfather James took out a land grant on what's now Hay Street, the main thoroughfare of Perth. He, his wife Elizabeth and five children arrived on the *Caroline,* the second ship to reach the new colony. A carpenter, he helped build the first government office building and then exchanged his land for another piece further up-river.

**Few of her possessions have survived, but Grandmother Lucy's pretty milk pitcher is one of them.**

Seven years later he died in an accident and was buried in a now-unmarked grave on the riverbank. He left his teenaged son Alfred to clear the land for Springpark Farm and build his mud-brick cottage in the heart of the Upper Swan District. The rest of the children gravitated toward the East taking their widowed mother with them.

In the infant colony of Swan River, so far away from the friendly old villages of south England, people had rather limited options. Was that why five Minchin brothers married five Hitchcock sisters—my grandparents among them? Is that therefore why our bonds of family friendship have bordered on clannishness ever since? Is that why we, even now at the third, fourth and fifth generations, still look enough alike to pass for siblings?

Pictures of one's pioneer ancestors can speak so eloquently. It wasn't just that the old processes of photography froze their faces in time. They stood stiffly in their Victorian clothes, ramrod straight and defiant in their tintype portraits for other reasons too. Look into their eyes. No be-flowered hat, nor celluloid collar, nor carved chair can mask the shadow of suffering, the knowledge of hardship and disappointment, the harsh realities of survival. Try as we may to understand, we really have little insight into the lives they lived.

Yet of such families as these Australia was made. Could our forebears look in on how we children have used the legacy they gave us, I think they might, for the most part, have approved—their solemn faces notwithstanding. Together the Minchins and Hitchcocks formed a numerous tribe in Western Australia.

While Uncle Len and his sister, Auntie Ruby, lived in the east, near Sydney, New South Wales, we had many relatives to visit in the West first. These included Uncle Vic and Uncle Harold, some other old aunts and uncles and innumerable quantities of cousins of all ages. All were eager to see us, and a busy round of teas greeted our arrival in Western Australia.

# CHAPTER 21

# Going Home to Australia

After the years in the Orient, I fell in love with Australia at first sight. Carnarvon, first port-of-call, clung to the coast of the northwest desert. A rangy cattle town, its dreary wood-frame houses slumbered behind their shabby verandahs. A few spindly gum trees provided shade here and there, like tired old men hoisting up their ragged umbrellas over the rambling settlement. Yet, I think, in all of my eleven years I'd never been quite so excited. Here I caught the atmosphere of a whole new world. Indeed, I imagined it to be one of the gates to Paradise itself.

While the crew loaded hundreds of beef cattle into the hold of our ship, passengers went ashore. Some visited the pubs. The rest of us simply walked the unpaved streets of the town. Nothing else to do and virtually nothing to look at. Yet something stirred within me, a kind of sensing of a hitherto unknown part of my heritage.

"Oh, Dad!" I pranced along at his side, thrilled to the very roots of my toenails. "I could just live here the rest of my life." Not that I'd been lonely among my Chinese, Indian and Malay friends back in Singapore, but here I saw dusty-faced, barefooted children who seemed to be essentially just like me. This discovery overwhelmed my imagination.

Dad looked down at me. "I think, Dottie … " He smiled one of his quizzical smiles and patted me on the head. "I think that you'd get rather tired of it after a while." I knew, of course, that he must be wrong, but the unfolding procession of events in this new land gave me neither time nor inclination to argue the point with him.

I spent hours at the rail watching the cowboys hustle the poor animals down the narrow chute with electric cattle prods. A little shot of electricity and the beasts stampeded down into the hold in a most satisfying way. They reminded me of the days when I chased chickens on Grandpa's farm in Iowa, but on a much grander scale. I loved the drama but didn't comprehend the fate awaiting them.

Every morning of our trip from Singapore I visited the ship's doctor to have my wounded knee dressed. That had not been fun. My bicycle accident the day before we left Singapore had left me with a mangled leg. The ship's doctor was a rough, semi-drunk old fossil who had little patience with anyone, least of all a frightened little girl. He dug the dead tissue out of my wound with all the delicacy of a miner drilling for oil. I knew instinctively that he wouldn't abide my resorting to anything so comforting as tears. Even after a week of misery, my knee didn't show so much as the beginnings of healing.

By now I found some rather tangible likenesses between him and the cattle prodders. Times I wasn't suffering in the hands of that doctor, I watched the cattle loading. I actually didn't realize that the cattle were destined for the slaughter houses of Perth. Reared in an essentially vegetarian household, I did not comprehend this fact at all.

The first morning we put to sea, we found the aft deck veiled from passenger view by huge tarpaulins. By squeezing my face through one of the cracks, I saw a horror I'd never dreamed of, the butchering of eight oxen. The carcasses hung from the yardarm, blood and gore making the deck slick. The crew members sweated in their greasy, black rubber aprons. I burst into tears.

A kindly man in a nearby deckchair tried to comfort me. "But they were hurt when they crashed down the passageway into the hold," he explained. "Their legs were broken. Besides, they'd all have to die soon anyway." I looked at my stiff knee with its oozy stain soaking through the bandage again. I couldn't understand why anyone ought to be killed just for having a bad leg. At dinner that night I saw "Ox-tail Soup" and "Braised Tongue" on the menu. It didn't make me feel any better.

Thinking of all the cattle jammed into the hold depressed me for the rest of the voyage. I shuddered at the thought of such a massive and universal appointment with death. I repented of my laughing at them when they'd thundered down the chute back in Carnarvon.

After a seventeen-year absence, Gerald spent a month visiting home-places around Perth, Western Australia. Rather unimpressed with the old relatives, Dorothy and Eileen amused themselves playing on the porch steps.

Very soon, however, life was going to become marvelously better.

After twenty days at sea, our ship docked in Fremantle, on Tuesday morning, April 8. My Dad hurried to greet the stranger who strode up the gangway to meet us. I know now what a deeply emotional moment that must have been the meeting of the two brothers after all of those many years. While my Dad was long and thin, Uncle Vic was more short and round. Otherwise, the two looked more like twins than just brothers.

# Chapter 22

# My Swan River Family

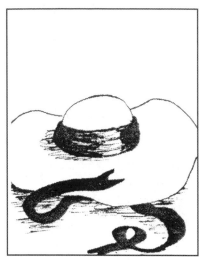

So we arrived at Uncle Vic's house on Queens Road in South Guildford. "Brentwood" opened its doors to us, and we became part of its family for several weeks. By this time in his life Uncle had become a gentleman farmer, visiting his Northam farm only as needed.

At this place I came to a whole new awareness of the World War. Formerly, it had meant just two things to me. Smart in his uniform, Dad supervised the Anti-Aircraft Defense Corps on the school campus in Singapore. We practiced blackouts and watched incendiary bombs detonate, so that the men could learn how to put out the fires.

Secondly, Dad spent at least an hour every evening listening to the BBC

Chosen, perhaps, for his British citizenship, Gerald Minchin (center, back row) became the chief officer of the Air Raid Precaution (ARP) Unit based on the school campus in Singapore. The men were trained to manage blackouts, apply first aid, and deal with incendiary bombs. Singapore confidently expected to defend itself from an attack from the sea. The Japanese, however, came in by the "back door" and the city fell in just one week (February 15, 1942).

broadcast from London on our shortwave radio. That's how we kept track of what the Germans were doing in Europe. I never understood much about it, except that I knew that Winston Churchill was a great statesman. That General Bernard Montgomery was a great hero. And, above all, that Hitler was a wicked man. I modeled clay figures of all three of them, in pink and green plasticine. Of course, there had been my nightly prayers that Hitler would die in his bed and get himself out of the way, but heretofore that had been the extent of my involvement in what everyone called the "War Effort."

In Australia things were more personal. I found that my own Cousin Gordon Minchin was in the RAAF (Royal Australian Air Force). They told me he was red-haired with freckles and that he was away at the war. His younger brother Ross, however, was only seventeen. He was working his first job in a chocolate factory. (Later he would be "man-powered" to work on his father's farm up at Jennacubbine.)

Uncle Vic and Aunt Agnes had had their second family, John and Ellen, ten years after Gordon and Ross. A couple of years my junior, the younger kids turned out to be admirable companions, ready and willing to join in any project afoot.

Aunt Agnes served marvelous meals at the dining table in what the family called the "vestibule" at the back of the house. These meals bore no resemblance to the rice, curry and tropical fruit salad on which I'd been reared. I loved the way the potatoes came out of the oven, swimming in a pool of thin brown gravy around a roast of mutton or beef. For some reason, I never connected any of that with the slaughtered cattle on the deck of the ship coming down from Carnarvon.

I was also inducted into the eating of trifle, a delicious mixture of cake, custard, cream, fruit and jello. Having originated in England, it had been tastily modified in Australia. In twenty-five years Aunt Agnes hadn't lost a syllable of the brogue she'd brought from Scotland, and she also served traditional hot scones with a variety of homemade jams and marmalades. But nothing—not even all these delicious things put together—equaled the marvel of lamingtons! Those cubes of sponge cake were dipped in chocolate and rolled in coconut. Sometimes they had jam and cream injected into their sweet little hearts. These were the masterpiece of Aunt Agnes's kitchen.

Because she always had the lamington tin on the pantry shelf filled, she had to keep her ear tuned for any predatory activities on the part of John and Ellen. Quite regularly, when the adults would be visiting in the front sitting room, Auntie would spring to her feet crying, "Och! And that's the lid of my lamington tin I hear."

Everyone would rush to the kitchen just in time to see John and Ellen fleeing down the garden path and on into the sheep paddock beyond, their hands full of lamingtons. I enjoyed listening to Uncle Vic standing on the back steps shouting after them, threatening them with annihilation if they didn't come back at once. They never came. They knew. He knew. We all knew that he couldn't chase them. Hours later, when they did come back, he'd have forgotten all about the charges he'd laid against them.

When Ross came home on Friday afternoons, however, the climate changed. He usually brought several pounds of broken chocolates as a treat for the family. Accustomed to leniency all week, John seldom could resist the temptation to help himself to Ross's chocolates. His theft-and-escape routine hardly ever succeeded. With the advantage of his long legs and youthful vitality, Ross easily overtook the miscreant and meted out judgment on the spot. He would simply wipe up the ground with John—and that without benefit of any mediation or court hearing.

Yet, with Ross absent most of the week, the habit was never really broken. Therefore, I too learned how to raise the lid of the lamington tin without a sound, and I could burn up the path to the paddock as swiftly as anyone else.

We had another war connection. Soldiers on leave, coming and going from camp or making their last visits before shipping out overseas, made constant use of the bus stop at the end of our street. We kids discovered a great many torn-up letters around the bench where the men sat waiting for the bus.

While John and Ellen didn't at first recognize the potential interest here, I pointed out to them that these were probably love letters. In the simplicity of our lives at that point, none of us had much idea of what such a letter might be like, but we did know how to find out. "Each of us will pick up all the pieces of one kind of paper and writing," I instructed my crew. What a stimulating way to spend a sunny winter morning, picking up handfuls of tom paper at the bus stop!

We took them home, spread newspapers on the parlor floor and made up some flour-and-water paste. Then we pieced the letters together, like puzzles. The results proved to be well worth the effort. Ellen couldn't read yet, but John and I willingly read the letters to her. We also interpreted them for her, as needed. Some were on lavender paper. Some smelled of perfume. All of them were so soggy and sentimental that they almost soaked through into Aunt Agnes's floral carpet. We didn't realize that people ever said stuff like that to each other. In fact, we had more fun with them than the Sunday comics. We were never at a loss to create good times for ourselves.

While in Perth, for the first time in my life, I had intimations of growing up and undergoing the process of becoming civilized. I would have to, within the foreseeable future, make the transition from childhood to adult life. With Aunt Agnes leading the way, I was swept along into the ladies' wear shops. Clothes the like of which I'd never seen in the tropics now confronted me. First, I was condemned—again—to wearing thick brown cotton stockings. Then came a knitted pink dress topped by a blue wool coat. I could barely remember ever having had a coat on in my life before.

The final indignity, however, was a pink felt hat that tied under my chin. I loathed all of it, but the hat above all. Providence had never yet answered my prayers for the privilege of having long hair. So, outrageously short boy-style haircuts still plagued my life. The wretched pink hat did absolutely nothing for the thick shock of sandy, dead-straight hair that protruded from beneath it.

Nonetheless, the weather was cold, and I couldn't reject all these woolen garments out of hand. Still, I had a certain pleasure of revenge upon The System in which I suffered. At this time I began to develop the art of concerning myself with everything else except what had to do with my appearance. A kind of an escape from enslavement. This attitude would cause my parents considerable concern before I turned the next corner in my adolescence. Trapped among so many physical besetments, I simply refused, for the next four years, to take an interest in hair, dress, or any other phase of fashion.

I also persisted, over-long, in talking Chinese English. A distinctive

**West Australian Missionary College (formerly Darling Range School) overlooking its apple orchards.**

dialect that I'd brought from Singapore. Even today, when I'm disposed to find a place to lay some blame, I remember that dreadful pink hat. I could probably find a psychologist somewhere to agree with my conviction that it actually did me emotional harm.

Meanwhile, our weeks in Western Australia afforded many diversions. We had some days with Uncle Harold and Auntie Maude. Because their children had all left home Eileen and I found little entertainment there. I did, however, have a chance to admire their son, my extraordinarily handsome Cousin Vernon Minchin. A few days after our arrival, he shipped out to duty in Europe. He was a navigator in the Royal Australian Air Force, and only a few months later his plane was shot down over Norway. He left behind a young widow and a baby boy whom he never saw. Now the war in Europe became painfully real, even to us kids.

Our family went to hosts of other relatives and innumerable churchyards so that Dad could enjoy his family, both the living and the dead. Being, as he always said, a "sentimental bloke," he savored every moment of the visits. To his birthplace in Cottesloe, between Peppermint Grove and the magnificent beach on the Indian Ocean. To his father's vineyard in Caversham, just across the Swan River from Guildford. To the Guildford Primary School and Perth Boys School. To his mother's grave at St. Mary's in the Middle Swan District. To To His Majesty's Theater in Perth where he heard his first concert. To Hillcrest

In 1941 the trans-Australian train steamed and hissed its way across the Nullabor Plain, seen only by a few desert Aboriginals and kangaroos. When the train stopped to take on water at an artesian well, Gerald Minchin took this picture of the engine that was hauling our family on the long west-to-east journey from Perth to Sydney.

Farm in South Caroling where he and Uncle Len rode their ponies, Ginger and Dolly, to school. And so on!

Finally we spent a weekend at the West Australian Missionary College (now Carmel College) to recapture his high school days. The school orchard grew the biggest, sweetest apples I've ever tasted, from that day to this.

Once again, Dad reconnected with his heritage, a son of those first settlers who emigrated from England to the Swan River Colony in 1829. We were all duly proud of our pioneer stock, but back there in 1941 I understood little of all this. From the start, I understood that we were descended from free settlers, not convicts. Times change, however, and nowadays being descended from convicts is, more or less, the Australian equivalent of belonging to the American Mayflower crowd!

During this first home-to-Australia visit I simply measured the quality of each encounter by the number of children or animals available for me to play with. With reluctance and considerable boredom, Eileen and I permitted old relatives to kiss us, pat us on our heads, and talk about us.

For my Dad, however, that had to be the very grandest of all grand home-comings ever enacted.

In due course, we embarked on the four-day train journey to Sydney. At every state line we had to change trains because the Australians had not yet agreed on what was the correct gauge for the railway tracks. The resulting variations, of course, consumed much time.

# CHAPTER 23

# The Cousin Encounter

Sixty-nine years ago, crossing the Australian desert bore little resemblance to today's luxury journey. Instead of the *Indian Pacific* streamliner streaking grandly across the Nullabor Plain where the track neither curves nor rises for almost 400 miles, our train dragged its old wooden carriages along. Still, the engine puffed and hissed and smoked in a most entertaining way. Each compartment was a kind of "dog box" with its own door opening to the outside.

For days, Eileen and I sat with our noses pressed to the window as we clacked across the desert. We watched for kangaroos, emus, and artesian wells. We stared, unblinking, at the old aboriginals with their boomerangs, crowding up to the train when the engine stopped to take on water and belch out steam.

Then one bright afternoon Uncle Len met us in Melbourne. He took us to attend a youth camp with him up in the mountains. Every night we shivered while we ate thick green pea soup in the drafty dining shed. Being cold turned out to be an entirely new sensation for Eileen and me.

Afterwards we took a day to play in the snows of the Dandenong Range above Warburton. Then, round-eyed, we took in the marvels of the city of Melbourne. There, for the first time, Eileen saw a horse. We found him, early in the wintry morning, hitched to a bakery wagon on Collins Street. "O look, Mummy!" Eileen pointed an agitated finger at the patient animal. "See the smoke coming out of that cow!"

The greatest wonder of all was yet to come. An event so staggering that it would make everything else subside into nothingness by comparison. The seven cousins—the Seven Little Australians, as we would come to call ourselves—were about to see one another for the first time. Along with Uncle

Len we boarded the very modern *Spirit of Progress* for the overnight journey from Melbourne to Sydney. The smooth, sleek train with its heated green floor hardly seemed even a distant relative to the iron horse of the desert that had carried us for all those days from Perth.

Even though I spent the whole night anticipating the moment of meeting The Cousins, the Sydney arrival still came with a jolt of surprise. I knew them, of course, the moment I looked through the window. The express train eased to a halt, placing me almost directly in front of the group of five, long-legged little kids. Kelvin in his short gray pants and striped school-tie, socks pulled up to his knobby knees. Skinny, wide-eyed Joan with her blond hair assiduously set in waves. (Now that really impressed me.) Brown-eyed Yvonne in her orange coat, a bit chunky-like me. And the twins, Valmae and Leona, with their long curly braids and thick black stockings, so alike that they might have come off a duplicating machine.

In the mountains of Victoria, the family encountered snow for the first time in six years. From left: Eileen, Leona Minchin, Len Minchin, and Dorothy.

I scrambled out onto the station platform, and we gravely looked one another over, in complete silence. Our reserves dropped almost immediately, though. Before we reached the suburban train, we'd forgotten our parents and had fallen to talking among ourselves. To be sure, life would never be the same for any of us again. Kelvin expounded on the Sydney Harbor Bridge as we crossed it, and the girls all made their own little conversational contributions as well. By the time we reached the Wahroonga station we felt perfectly at ease.

So much so, that as we turned off Fox Valley Road and down Douglas Avenue, all was, indeed, right with our world.

When Uncle Len and Auntie May had finished building their new little house, they named it *Kirambee* meaning in the Aboriginal language, "Happy Home." Living up to its name, it now enfolded us all—both families—as if it had been expressly built for just such a reunion day.

Even before we ate lunch, the cousins escorted Eileen and me around the premises to show us the really important features of the place. First came Cousin Jess's tent in the back yard. (Jess Laird, daughter of Dad's eldest sister, was a survivor of the tuberculosis that had destroyed her family years before. Outdoor living was the best prescription for TB anyone knew of at that time.)

Then we saw the cow. She was called Sally, a name that had been hastily substituted for Belle, my mother's second name. The association had been deemed unfit. All the same, neither children nor cow had yet become accustomed to the new name. Then we visited Fluffy, a magnificent gray Persian cat, and called in on the chooks (chickens). Next, we cased out The Shack down at the back of the garden, a place with extra beds for extra people. In fact, while *Kirambee* had been under construction, that tin shed had housed the entire family.

The climax of the sightseeing tour, however, was the dugout, an impressive underground retreat built by Kelvin. He began it as a bomb shelter, for he'd been quite concerned by all the war propaganda. Now he'd converted it into a clubhouse for our amusement, a major engineering achievement actually. Indeed, we very promptly began club business in there. Inside the house we examined Cousin Verna's room. (Verna Britten was Auntie Ruby's daughter who worked as a secretary in Sydney. By living here, she combined the independence of her career with the companionship of her family.)

Then we examined Eileen's little bed that had been added to the master bedroom. (Uncle Len and Auntie May had vacated the room to sleep down in The Shack.) Kelvin's bed was set amid the books in his father's study.

Finally, most enticing of all, we came to the long back verandah, the "Sleep Out."

Here we five girls would be together. I'd been an only child for a long time. Eight years younger than I, Eileen hadn't yet counted for much in the way of companionship.

I'd long dreamed of being in the heart of a large family. So now I could hardly wait until night so that we could go to bed. I wanted to find out what it was like to sleep in a room full of girls.

Certainly, any anxieties our parents may have had about our compatibility could have been laid to rest by the end of that very first day. Even now I can't seem to recall one time when any of us really quarreled, then or ever after.

Our cousin encounter that day scored a total success.

# CHAPTER 24

# The Little Missions at School

My delight in discovering my Australian cousins was at first a little tempered by the necessity of breaking into a new elementary school. Fortunately, I became thoroughly embedded in life at Uncle Len's house. So much so, that when Dad, Mum and Eileen moved up north to Avondale to a new house and new work, I scarcely noticed them leave. Dad had a new job as vice-principal of his old school, Australasian Missionary College. Probably a few tears on my part would have been appropriate, but I had none to shed. I was going to stay with the cousins and finish out the school year. Nothing else really mattered.

At the same time, entering Grade 6 in Wahroonga Primary School halfway through the year challenged all that I had to give. Occasionally more than I had to give.

With that wise insight that long-time, good teachers always seem to acquire, Miss Veronica Camp assigned me to share a desk with Joan. Directly in front of us sat Kelvin and Cleve Bateman. Over against the far wall, in Grade 4, Yvonne had her desk. Immediately next-door were the twins in Grade 1. In addition to simply looking alike, they already exhibited other curious likenesses that identical twins may have. Valmae and Leona, for instance, could earn the same score on a test and still make their mistakes in different places.

I, on the other hand, had no distinctive features to augment my introduction to the school. While I proved to be well ahead in reading and writing and while I almost popped the buttons off my school blazer when Miss Camp read one of my essays in class, I stood well below the survival level in maths. Very young and very new, I didn't fit anywhere during those first weeks. All of Miss Camp's patience, kindness and careful attention couldn't hide the fact from me.

Moreover, having grown up among Americans and Chinese, I didn't sound like an Australian. This deficiency put me into real jeopardy out in the school-yard at recess time. Besides, I knew nothing about playing cricket, and I always tripped myself and fell whenever I tried to skip rope "doubles."

Things could be tough with my every move scrutinized by my betters. One day I picked up a dirty handkerchief in the hall. I could see that it was pretty but obviously lost. Promptly Judy told me I wasn't a Christian for doing that. Then two of the Grade 9 boys called me a football and laughed at me. For a long time, I found my identity only in the loves and loyalties of my cousins. Six Minchins in two classrooms provided power of numbers and a security that comforted me,

When another missionary child came to school, even later than I, she came to recognize the strength of our superior forces. Being totally deaf, Verna Mae had learned to hold her own by sheer muscle-power.

One day before he headed north, my Dad had come down to the schoolyard to take a picture of the six of us. Being ranged according to age confirmed our family unity. With Kelvin at the head of the line of girls we

The Minchin cousins styled themselves the "Seven Little Australians" (after a popular book of the day). Six of them presented a solid front at the Wahroonga Primary School. Left to right: Kelvin, Dorothy, Joan, Yvonne, Valmae and Leona (the twins).

**Pre-schooler Eileen spent her days at home, dreaming of the day when she would come into her own.**

stood proud and straight in our school uniforms. Then Verna Mae crowed, "See all those Missions (Minchins) getting their picture taken." Everyone in the schoolyard stopped to look at us. Somehow the episode conferred a kind of dignity upon us and gave us a certain status in the school.

A husky twelve-year-old, Verna Mae Hare asserted herself the first week by swinging around and catching me with a right hook that almost knocked me out cold on the floor. That happened during singing class.

Taken by surprise, I sang out a little louder than I intended. Miss Camp promptly sent the girl home with a note. The next day her father brought her back. Master-storyteller that he was, Eric B. Hare pacified us all by telling thrilling stories from Burma. As it turned out, Verna Mae meant no real harm.

Our family has always been, if nothing else, a rather creative one. Considering, therefore, the potential for mischief that we had among us, we actually got into relatively little trouble at school. For us girls, our misdemeanors, when aligned with those of most of our schoolmates, were quite mild. Kelvin and Cleve, on the other hand, knew the path to the headmaster's door rather well.

We extravagantly admired Kelvin's ingenuity. We knew the place in the bush where he picked up cicadas to carry to school. He'd hide one in the folds of his school tie, all decently tucked into his gray sweater. Then, when a proper atmosphere of silent scholarship pervaded in the classroom, he'd press the appropriate part of the insect's anatomy and the rhythmic music would begin, almost under Miss Camp's nose. It had been no accident, of course, that she'd seated Kel and Cleve directly in front of her own desk. In any case, a reckless lifestyle was rather the expected thing for the boys.

One morning, however, a visitor to morning worship was responsible for sending Joan and me up to judgment in the principal's office. After a long talk, the guest prayed a very long prayer, an interminably long prayer. Finally, Joan and I simultaneously opened our eyes. Under the desk we saw, within easy reach, the four soles of Kelvin's and Cleve's shoes. The boys themselves we noted, were making paper-and-pen-nib darts under their desk, ammunition for use later in the day. They always kept a supply on hand.

Obviously Miss Camp herself had her eyes open too. So she spotted us writing names on the bottoms of the boys' shoes with chalk. For that we were sent to see the principal. He administered no corporal punishment. Indeed, none was needed. Amid all our tears Joan and I were utterly crushed with the ignominy of the whole affair. Joan's slate was so righteous, so absolutely clean of wrong doing, that she could hardly endure the shame. In contrast, I was shattered not so much because of injured innocence but because I was trying so hard just to fit in and be accepted. Nonetheless, I too suffered near-mortal grief that day. How was I going to make both the kids and the teachers like me?

Before noon, however, Kel and Cleve were sent up to the same judgment throne for having activated their darts a little too recklessly. I watched them go. They walked off to their punishment like heroes, smiling! How I envied them! I even envied them the caning they got, for that in itself meant that they were securely *in*.

# CHAPTER 25

# Membership in the Secret Society

Home at *Kirambee* was situated about a mile from the school. The first path we walked took us through the bush, up onto Fox Valley Road, past Fletcher's Store. Then we went on toward the Sanitarium. On the way we passed the big brick office building where Uncle Len worked. Then, one more bend down into the bush again, and we stood in front of the Wahroonga Primary School.

The road offered many diversions, and the journey to school could be very time-consuming. Two palm trees in front of Uncle's office produced an odd fruit that tasted like a cross between pineapple and coconut. We vied with one another to see who could eat the most. (As if Auntie hadn't already filled us up with steamed granola for our breakfast that morning!) A lantana hedge ran along the front of the office building. We gathered its blossoms, showering one another with a rain of pink, yellow and lavender petals or stuffing them down the backs of one another's school uniforms. On the opposite side of the street stood what we called our "Lilly Pilly Tree." It bore little red-marble berries.

As our Cousin League solidified, we found it necessary to follow certain secret proceedings. First came the invention of a new language with which we could communicate with one another when we got caught in the presence of our parents or were otherwise surrounded by the enemy. Although the language was nothing more than simple Pig Latin, it was exceedingly important to us at the time.

Then we created a kind of loyalty oath known as "The Sentence," followed by certain highly classified secret passwords. We recorded everything carefully in a little black book.

Presently our organization began to show the strain of the class distinctions that had developed. To some degree, our ages dictated this segregation. Except for Eileen, we'd all been born within a period of less than five years. At the time, however, that made a significant difference. The twins, naturally, always went together, and whenever Eileen came around she was allotted to their department. At the other end of the scale, Kelvin, Joan and I stood with less than two years among us.

That left Yvonne squarely in the middle. Not that she was actually excluded from either camp. It was just that no one had any clear clue as to where she belonged. Despite her nebulous position, we employed her actively in all on-going projects. Rarely do children spend a lot of time worrying about how other children feel, so Yvonne was probably the only one in the gang who gave the situation much thought. Later years, however, would reveal that she had felt excluded. So when in doubt, she set herself up as Eileen's primary champion. She shone in the role of defending the baby of the family and thus acquired an identity.

Another vital enterprise of our "Mission Organization" was to hew a new track out of the bush, known as The *Rackta* (pronounced rak-tay). It enabled us to proceed to school in a totally secret and private way, along a path entirely unknown to the common people about the neighborhood.

Who knows where we got the idea! Perhaps we picked it up on the evenings when we had to crash through the bush down to Brown's Pasture, hunting for Sally to bring her home for her evening milking.

Whatever the motivation, we did carve out a trail worthy of the pioneers. It had secret hideaways along the sides and specially marked trees under which we recited incantations from the Black Book. Rock arrangements and messages left in tin cans by the path enabled us to communicate with one another whenever we walked the trail separately.

Another obligation had to do with kissing the large knot on the tree named "Pinehane" and touching our foreheads to the fork in the tree we called "Pinehurst." It's hard to know where we gleaned our ideas for all of these rituals. Perhaps some Druidic forest practices from our long-ago Celtic ancestors somehow filtered down to us.

At first, we didn't initiate Valmae and Leona into the "Brotherhood of

The Rackta." Wary as leopards, we'd stand in one of our hideouts and watch
them walking the public path below. For a long time we considered them too
young, but finally the unity of the Club proved to be more important than a
mere age gap. So, with secret ceremonies, we inducted them into our mysteries. Their brown eyes full of wonder, they joined us, never questioning why
they'd had to wait so long to be accepted. Then, we even gave Eileen a tour of
our fantasyland. The three younger members made such satisfying and agree-
able followers! All chiefs, as everyone knows, must have at least a few Indians.

The next duty we imposed upon our membership involved finding a
stone as soon as we emerged from The Rackta onto the paved road. Better
still, we should find a suitable stone in the little grassy paddock just before we
reached the road. Then we had to kick the stone all the way to school, without
ever touching it or picking it up. If the stone should roll over the bank and
become inaccessible, then it was permissible to pick it up in a handkerchief and
set it on the sidewalk again. The latter measure naturally detracted from the
excellence of the overall performance and was to be avoided, if at all possible.

Needless to say, our shoes very quickly began to show unusual wear.
Being committed to so much secrecy, however, we had no way of explaining

Today, trees have grown up around *Kirambee* on Douglas Avenue, Wahroonga. Much lived-
in and much loved, the house often enfolded all eleven of the family at one time.

to our inquiring parents why our shoes were deteriorating so fast. For two reasons, this matter could not be taken lightly. First, there simply wasn't money available for extras—and sometimes barely enough for necessities. Second, we all have very big feet, large to the point of deformity. At the time however, we girls—even the twins—took great pride in buying our shoes in the women's instead of children's shoe departments. That meant more money, of course.

All of these considerations notwithstanding, the stone kicking remained of prime importance. We even did it in our best shoes on the way to church, if we had the good fortune to be walking unsupervised.

Then we shouldered yet another responsibility. We had to avoid stepping on any cracks in the sidewalk. (We knew them to be poison.) Indeed, the trip from *Kirambee* to school or church could be a very onerous journey. It took a lot of time and energy.

One other pastime for the road, fortunately, did not become a permanent part of our club structure. One day, we took chalk from school, and as we passed the high wooden fence near Uncle's office, we wrote our names (including the family name) along with a few other comments on the weathered boards. Later, when Uncle himself walked home, he saw the writing. He arrived at tea (supper) that night wearing a very serious face. He was not amused, and he gave us good and sufficient reason for not committing that crime again, ever.

Our secret society bonded us so thoroughly that we supported one another, without question, even in the most threatening circumstances. Lack of a telephone in the house necessitated Auntie May's sending us older girls, one night, over to Ada Avenue where Uncle Albert (our fathers' cousin) and Auntie Doll lived. Things had pretty well settled down for that night in the Sleep Out when the call came.

Although Auntie delivered the note to Joan, Yvonne, me, the twins saw a chance to delay bedtime and begged to go too. Then Kelvin, with a touch of scorn, suggested that "all yous girls" probably shouldn't be out in the dark alone, and he offered to go also. All of us in our pajamas, we rolled up the legs, put on our long winter coats and buttoned them up snugly.

Thus, in a band, we climbed the hill to Fox Valley Road, no one admitting fear but all clinging to one another because of the cold. We walked the half-mile, running through the dark shadows between the streetlights. In one of those lonely passages, two St. Bernard dogs rushed out upon us. We knew they'd be there, but they looked so much larger at night than in the daytime! We ran in a panic, and most of our pajama legs fell down.

Soon we stood on the porch of Uncle Albert's house, desperately trying to hide our drooping pajama-legs again. We'd been given this responsibility—and at night too—and we were determined to carry it out in an adult way. Our sleepwear had seemed all right when we left home, but now it detracted considerably from the dignity of our mission. Uncle Albert opened the door, and the six of us trouped in to where a bright fire blazed on the grate.

"Won't you take off your coats and stay a little while?" Auntie Doll inquired. "I have some little cakes, fresh baked this afternoon."

Although we'd begun to perspire in our coats, we couldn't think of missing the cakes. Besides, Uncle and Auntie talked to us, not like children, but like real people. The evening, in fact, evolved into a social event in which we felt very grown up. So we made conversation politely for some time, eating sweets daintily, and sweating profusely inside our woolen coats.

Unfortunately we didn't know how to end the visit. How in the world do you leave gracefully? There had to be some way to do it! We looked at one another anxiously, excruciatingly aware of our slipping pajama bottoms.

Finally, Yvonne broke the spell. Prone to twisting words, she announced, "Well, I bes we getter go home now." We all stood up on the signal and headed for the front door in a body, barely registering her *faux pas*. Now, oh joy, we could leave!

On the threshold, I felt my right pajama leg slither all the way down to my ankle. I looked back in time to see Uncle Albert and Auntie Doll exchange knowing, adult smiles. Feeling very much like children again, we scurried back down Fox Valley Road, the two dogs chasing us part of the way. Fallen pajama legs didn't matter any more.

Next morning we reviewed the previous night. We decided that Yvonne's "sentence of dismissal" had proved an effective formula and could, therefore, be used for future needs. We entered "I bes I getter go" into our Black Book.

We set other goals for ourselves too. Every trip to Sydney challenged our highest powers. With far more zeal that we ever felt for learning dates in history class, we set ourselves to memorizing the names of all the suburban railway stations between Wahroonga and Wynyard Station in the heart of Sydney—Warrawee, Turramurra, Killara, Pymble, Gordon, and so forth. It was a question of who could call out the name of the next station first. The twins, though still quite limited in their reading vocabulary, liked to join in.

On one occasion we older ones, the bosses, couldn't remember the name of the next station. Somehow we even missed the station sign itself. Then, eager and helpful, Leona's voice piped through the train. "Oh, I know the name of this station. It's spelled "L-A-D-I-E-S!"

Milson's Point marked the north end of Sydney Harbor Bridge. Arriving there meant that we had to draw a long, deep breath, because when we passed the massive pylons at the end of the bridge we couldn't breathe again until we reached the far end. Usually about three-quarters of the way across, we'd be struggling to hold out, the distance being just a shade too much for us. We'd hang on until we turned blue. Once in a while one of us managed to make it all of the way. As the train shot through the southern gateway of the bridge, the winner would almost collapse into the aisle. Then, trembling from oxygen depletion, we'd all sit up and grin at each other. We loved doing hard things—if we could choose them for ourselves.

I can find no plausible explanation for the existence of our secret society, nor for our do-or-die adherence to all of its nonsensical rites. Child development experts tell us that such arrangements are not unusual at this age.

More than that, however, I like to think of the good it did us. The secrecy, the code of honor, the many all-absorbing projects, the demanding tasks, the loyalty to the group. All of these things helped to bond our love forever. It taught us a lot about the meaning of friendship. Furthermore, we practiced setting and accomplishing goals, no matter how trivial. We learned the meaning of teamwork.

Ultimately, we gained an enormous and vigorous sense of belonging.

# CHAPTER 26

# The Little Missions at Home

There were, I suppose, several reasons for the vast contentment that I enjoyed while living in Wahroonga. For the first time in my life I was really part of a big family. Under these idyllic circumstances, my imagination and academic abilities both began to blossom out in surprising ways.

After Dad and Mum moved to Avondale, Joan, Yvonne and I left the twins alone in the Sleep Out and moved into the master bedroom. A pleasant enough arrangement, except that while two of us slept in the double bed, the third one had to use a cot. For safety's sake, we pushed the cot as close as possible to the big bed. Still, it stood three or four inches lower, giving the sleeper a dismal sense of isolation and insecurity.

Trying to be cheerful about the situation, we took turns in the hazardous cot, recognizing the very real danger that lay in Kelvin's predatory tendencies. Sometimes at night he inserted a cardboard "head" in our window to impersonate a Peeping Tom. He also wired up mechanisms to make things fall out of the wardrobe upon our unsuspecting heads. He would even sacrifice hours of his own sleep to hide under the beds and pull the bedclothes off of us just as we were dozing off to sleep.

While all of these activities kept us in a perpetual panic, we loved it and would have been very sorry if he had deserted us. Some well-meaning people pitied Kelvin for being a boy alone among six sisters and girl-cousins. Indeed, he himself had, at times, been quite vocal on the subject. Everyone might well have laid all their anxieties and sympathies to rest, for he had a remarkable talent not only for holding his own but also for keeping us in total subjection to himself

First, I admired him for his feats of daring and for his ability to cope with dramatic situations. If a given situation were not sufficiently dramatic of itself, he knew how to make it so. One weekend he went camping with some boys and returned home with a broken tailbone. The doctor forbade him to sit down for six weeks.

Instead of bewailing his affliction, he used it for self-betterment and status improvement. At school he became a public hero as he stood hour after hour writing his lessons on top of the classroom lockers. At home, he reclined on a day bed like a Roman patrician while the rest of us ate at the dining table, vying with one another to wait upon his every need. Also, he continued to ride his bicycle—without sitting down, of course. Transfixed we watched him set off one morning to deliver four dozen eggs to Fletcher's Store. The fact that he fell off the bike at the top of Douglas Avenue and smashed all the eggs in no wise diminished him in our adoring eyes. Indeed, when he arrived home, completely attired in egg yolk and broken shells, we admired his uniqueness all the more.

We'd all been brought up to eating only the cleanest and most conservative of foods. Therefore, it was in matters of diet that Kel discovered his greatest power over us. One night in the laundry room, before our wondering eyes, he ate three of the cat's savaloys. We sat in a row on the cold wood stove and watched him do it! Savaloys looked like ordinary sausages, but they were made up of the refuse out of the butcher shop. So low-grade was the meat that a high-class cat like Fluffy sometimes didn't even care to eat them.

His most memorable effort occurred on a day when we children were at the table alone. On his lettuce he found a worm— a very complete, green, well-crafted worm. We all

**Ever the entrepreneur, Kelvin held his own. Even after he injured his back and couldn't sit for six weeks, he figured out how to ride his bicycle all over town— without touching the seat.**

drew back with appropriate whimpers of feminine reticence. "Do you want to see me eat this worm?" Kelvin looked around the table in a deceptively offhand manner.

It wasn't that we actually wanted to see him eat the worm. It was more that we just couldn't stand the deprivation of not seeing him do it. Then, with his usual aplomb, Kelvin made us each agree to give him sixpence out of our savings for the privilege of viewing the performance. Sixpence was a princely sum, and we debated the sacrifice that he demanded.

In the end we had to give in. Then, when we'd all, even the twins, had entered into the covenant to his satisfaction, he enfolded the worm, still couched on the lettuce leaf, into his sandwich. He calmly ate, savoring our tremulous little gasps of horror the while. No doubt he felt amply repaid for his labor, having received two shillings and sixpence from us. Yes, Kelvin always knew what worked. He had, I believe, the basic instincts of a true entrepreneur.

On Friday afternoons we helped Auntie May clean house. The best part of that service was polishing the linoleum in the dining room. We'd apply the wax liberally and then drag each other around under the table and out into the hall on the floor cloths. Our own bottoms made effective floor polishers, even though at times we put the furniture in jeopardy, laughing and squealing all the while. Auntie May never interfered with our methods. She decided, I suppose, that silly help was better than no help at all! .

I don't believe we ever had a dull mealtime. In the mornings, carefree and full of nonsense, we gobbled up our Weetabix and milk. Always hot milk for Yvonne, I remember. Then came the Marmite and bread, followed by jam and bread and the boiled cream  that was skimmed off of Sally's daily pan of milk.

Then we'd grab our lunch sacks and scamper off to school. Every night we had to pack our lunches for the next morning. Our sandwiches may have lacked gourmet quality, but some of them were unique: Cucumber and butter, dates and coconut, peanut butter and banana, even beetroot and cold potato. Always lots of peanut butter, mixed creamy smooth with warm water.

I learned in those days that if a substance is edible then it can be incorporated into a sandwich. I understand now, that that was the general idea Lord

Sandwich had in mind when he invented the convenient device for his hunting expeditions. Although I didn't care for the way the beets would bleed into the bread and turn it pink, I found grated carrots and raisins quite delicious together in a sandwich.

I believe we invented the Marmite-and-lettuce sandwich ourselves. Marmite is an acquired taste. We'd all been conditioned from childhood, however, and most of us ate that famous yeast product black on our bread. As I recall, our classmates sometimes eyed our sandwiches with curiosity, but we never cared what they thought about what they saw.

In the evening, we had tea (supper) at a more leisurely pace. Always a rousing good time, in spite of all the vegetables we had to eat because they were "good for us." Then, as always, there were those children starving in India.

Few desserts came our way, except on very special occasions. When the unusual did happen, we often had sago (a type of tapioca) pudding with lemon sauce. At first a treat and then later a bore, that food was labeled the "Everlasting Pudding." Even after what seemed hours of eating, the volume remained undiminished.

Afterwards, we filed from the supper table to the living room for evening worship, a regular appointment for the family. Uncle always went straight to the piano, and in moments the rafters rang with our singing. Our lusty voices would have done credit to a vast, outdoor campmeeting. We repeated our favorites day after day, month in and month out. Music seemed to be such a natural taste for all of us. Eileen had picked up a broad Australian accent within days of our arrival, and every night you could hear her shrill little voice, in perfect tune, singing "Sweeping Through the Gytes to the New Jer-u-sa-a-lem."

The evening dishwashing fell to us girls. None of us wanted to do it, of course, but we kept the competition so lively that even that task could be fun. If the washer didn't keep at least one item on the counter at all times, the wipers could, by agreement, walk off the job. I am surprised that so few of Auntie's dishes actually got broken. They were china too—ivory with a wreath of maple leaves around the rim and a twisted green-and-gold rope band at the edge. Plastic dinnerware being virtually unknown, we treasured any plastic containers like the crown jewels. China and glass were just the everyday stuff.

Our sleeping arrangements were somewhat fluid. Sometimes the twins slept down in the "Cubby Hole," an excavation under the house with a low, narrow door and a single window. They fit into the single bed and compensated for their isolation by being surrounded by all of the doll beds. This place was, in fact, the official play-house. After you'd changed half a dozen dolls into their nighties and tucked them into bed, you weren't so likely to remember to be scared.

When the master-bedroom was needed to accommodate greater persons than ourselves or when Uncle and Auntie themselves decided to sleep there, we older girls would move down to The Shack. A very cold place it was, enclosed only by corrugated iron and lacking electricity.

Still, the candles had their own pleasures to offer. We dripped the hot wax on our arms and legs and then picked it off after it became hard. A somewhat painful but nonetheless interesting going-to-bed entertainment.

The fact that we never set the beds on fire and burned down The Shack is, I am sure, due to the direct intervention of Providence.

# CHAPTER 27

# Homely Hazards

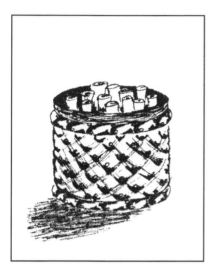

Some of our other household arrangements also made our lives period pieces at this time.

For example, a variety of activities went on in the laundry room. Auntie May baked her bread there, preferring the wood stove to the electric one upstairs. That's where Fluffy mothered her kittens.

Also, Auntie owned an electric washing machine. This fact, of itself, set our household apart from most of the neighbors. We all had detailed instruction on how not to crush our fingers in the wringer. Even so, this wonderful labor-saving device didn't eradicate all of the distress of doing laundry for a large family.

To the best of my knowledge, Kleenex hadn't yet been invented. Or, if it had, buying it would have been entirely out of the question for our frugal lifestyle. Consequently, everyone had his or her own box of handkerchiefs. Indeed, we took pride in our collections, with birthdays and Christmas always bringing in new prizes.

Winter colds raged among us, of course, with the result that washday presented an unspeakably nasty heap of dirty hankies. Even we kids could understand, however, that this slimy, sodden mass could not be tossed into the washing machine along with the other laundry. Which meant, then, that someone had personally, with her own bare hands, to pre-wash the hankies. While mucous is a necessary body fluid, the memories of that stiff, odiferous pile of dirty handkerchiefs every week still bring me very specific and sensory kinds of recall.

As the relatively unskilled laborers in the family organization, however, we girls had to do the chore. Ironing the hankies later was, of course, no problem. We enjoyed carefully folding each one and segregating the colorful

Kelvin, however, and Joan was voted down.

We got a ruler to measure and then filled the deep tub to sixteen inches. After a while, amid a great deal of splashing and jumping in and out, we realized that we had almost as much water out on the floor as in the tub. Wholly abandoned now to our revels, we filled the tub to the top and let the twins in too. "That allows us another eight inches, you know!" Kelvin grinned as he turned on the tap full tilt. "So we can just keep filling it all the way up, even if we do spill some."

After another half hour we were cool, contented and worn out. Only then did we realize that the bathroom looked like the final days of Noah's flood. We used up almost every towel in the linen cupboard trying to dry it up.

As for the rationed water? It was gone. That night, to be sure, we needed to pray with extra fervor that there should come "rain in the Catchment Area."

A peculiarity of Australian bathrooms in those days was that people thought it improper to have the toilet inside the house, in the usual place where one would expect to find that fixture today. Something to do with health. So the toilet at *Kirambee* was lodged in solitary splendor downstairs by the laundry room.

A run down the long ramp from the back door, a hairpin turn to the left, and a trot down a path bordered with banks of Wandering Jew plants brought you to a little porch. Straight ahead, past the tools and crates of garden stuff, lay the Cubby Hole, our play-house. To the right, however, you found the toilet—a noble machine with an iron tank very high overhead, a long chain hanging from one end, and a roar like Niagara Falls.

By day, negotiating a trip to the "lav" (toilet) posed no problem. Because of the length of the journey, however, one had to learn to judge his or her need accurately. Night-time brought additional difficulties. That was when those dark shapes in the shadows of the porch took on a life of their own. Our fears easily overwhelmed us. Certainly, no one wanted to make the gloomy pilgrimage alone. Moreover, the lighting was very bad.

Therefore, everyone's anxiety at bedtime was not to be left alone down there amid the terrors of the unknown. We developed an honor system that we took very seriously. We voted on the order of our going. The one who said,

"I bags first," would, without question, go first, accompanied by numbers two, three, four and five, in proper order.

To say "I bags" was, indeed, a very solemn commitment, and, in general, the arrangement worked. Because Joan could run faster than Yvonne and I, however, she sometimes violated the sacred sequence of events. Surprising in one who otherwise could be counted on to hold to the highest moral standards.

The twins, of course, always had each other and were fairly well equipped to be independent of the "bagsing" operation altogether, if things got out of hand. The real trauma always came when the last two wayfarers got left down there alone,

The "Twinnies" (Valmae and Leona) appeared in several weddings as flower girls. Obviously, they were beautifully designed for that role.

tied to each other in their extremity. The one having to stand outside by herself among the bogey-men suffered the most. There simply wasn't room for two persons to get into the toilet at one time.

All of these concerns, notwithstanding, the big family continued cheerful, healthy and prosperous. Whether Uncle and Auntie shared this precise viewpoint at all times is probably open to question. They certainly did have a lot of responsibility.

Still, we kids lived a life in those carefree months that, even now, I believe none of us can fault. Not one of us, I believe, would trade a single facet of any of our memories for a piece of anyone else's childhood, however exotic it might be.

# CHAPTER 28

# Living in the Laurels

With the end of the school year, I moved up north to our new home at Avondale College. My family came down to Wahroonga to get me, and for the first time, I made the three-hour train journey along the Hawkesbury River. The gorgeous scenery meant little to me. I was suffering the painful regret at leaving *Kirambee* and facing the terrible unknown connected with having to enter another new school. This time alone and without the support of my Secret Society.

We reached Dora Creek railway station and boarded old Mrs. Andersen's bus to go out to the college. A wizened-up, white-haired little crone, she had been driving the bus longer than anyone could remember. She ran a simple schedule. Twice a day she bumped over the corrugated roads in a teeth-loosening journey between the railway station and the college. And so, in the cool shadows of the evening, she delivered us, conveniently, right at the door of our house on College Avenue.

We lived on the first floor of "The Laurels," a barney-looking, two-storey house built by an imaginative American. It didn't look like any of the other conventional Australian houses on the street. The elegant name, I suppose, had reference to some camphor laurel trees that must have once stood in the front yard.

Savoring the sweetness of his homeland, Dad had fallen to gardening—something I'd never before seen him do, except for those almost forgotten days in Chariton, Iowa. At the back he had strawberries planted by the wash-shed, almost under the windows of the girls dormitory. He had mounted a swing under the huge eucalyptus tree that housed great families of kookaburras. In the front yard, he made rings of nasturtiums around the pair of gum trees that guarded our front doorstep. From Auntie Ruby, Dad's older sister, I soon

Brother and sister: E.L. Minchin and Ruby Minchin-Britten. Beloved Auntie Ruby not only mothered her early-orphaned brothers and her own children but also many nieces and nephews.

"Auntie Ruby's house" on Cooranbong Road was always a prime destination for Dorothy and Eileen. Through the ti-tree woods and Amen Gate and we arrived!

learned that nasturtium leaves made good sandwiches! Truly, I have never known a family more creative than ours in the matter of original recipes for sandwiches.

Inside the house were some—not many—pieces of new furniture. I liked the warm, autumn-toned Chesterfield (sofa) set. Because of the heat in Singapore, we'd had only teak-and-rattan furniture. Therefore, I found the overstuffed sofa and chair quite novel—even prestigious—especially in our house, of all places.

Little Eileen had missed me and had been, for weeks, eagerly anticipating my arrival. I found, happily, that her transition from three to four years old during my absence had given her a new independence. In fact, Mum told me that Eileen had personally supervised the furnishing of our little bedroom. It turned off at the end of a long hallway with its door set diagonally. For some unknown reason I found this little irregularity quite entrancing.

By now Eileen had graduated out of her cot and into one of the new twin beds. Moreover, Mum had bought us each a new, cloud-light blue eiderdown comforter for the cold nights. The oil stove in the kitchen and the

to walk the public trail without taking possession of any part of the bush-land around it. This may well have been an early symptom, a single, isolated clue that someday we'd have to grow up.

That winter brought us a large, unexpected group of visitors—all of our American missionary friends from Singapore. A few months earlier, when we'd stood on the deck of our departing ship and said our goodbyes, Mum and Dad had called out, "Come and visit us in Australia."

"Sure, we'll come," everyone shouted back. But how serious could that lot of Americans be about coming to Australia? Not much. The course of the war, however, gave them little choice.

Although Singapore had been fortified seaward, the Japanese army moved quickly overland and attacked from the rear. Our friends had only hours to escape, and the city fell in mid-February, 1942. Warplanes bombed their ship in Indonesia, and they went on with only the clothes they wore that day.

Finally, the refugee party arrived in Sydney. After weeks of privation and uncertainty, they thoroughly enjoyed the feast they had at the Sanitarium Café in Sydney. Indeed, before they all reached Avondale, I heard about how my friend, Buddy Bohner, had astonished all the locals along the way by the enormous amount of food he'd put away.

Being something of celebrity now, Buddy made me very proud to show him around Avondale. Still, two important people were missing from the group—my Uncle Gus Youngberg and Buddy's father, Len Bohner. Both of them had been imprisoned in Japanese concentration camps—one in Borneo and the other in French Indo-China (Vietnam). The first one would die, but the second would survive. Sadly, beyond that, soon after Len Bohner finally did get home again to the United States, his only son Buddy would die of polio at age eighteen.

None of those things could have affected us that May weekend in 1942. We kids simply reveled our way through our big party out on the lawn under the big gum tree where the kookaburras lived. Faculty women helped Mum feed the crowd. In the excitement of the moment, I even ate some watermelon before I realized what I was doing!

One way and another, our family settled into life at "The Laurels." Eileen and I were both entranced with the built-in breakfast-nook in the kitchen. We'd never known anything but loose chairs and tables. Sometimes very loose. Somehow, sliding into the benches made us think of some public and important occasion, like eating in a restaurant. Not that we had much knowledge. The only restaurant-eating we knew was once in a very long while going down to the Sanitarium Cafe on Hunter Street in Sydney. Assuredly, such things weren't a regular part of our lives. So the Laurels' breakfast nook had a charm all of its own, a magic that can't quite be described.

The benches and table were set on two sides by two windows, at right angles. The third side was a wall and a cupboard under the staircase going up to Miss Walker's rooms upstairs. We never saw much of her. A maiden lady of very long standing, she found children totally baffling. So we kept out of her way and she out of ours.

The breakfast-nook windows opened onto a screened verandah, a fine place for sitting in the evening when the kookaburras came out, perched in the gum trees and scolded us. A few chairs and a very tired old daybed made up the porch furnishings. It served as an out-of-the-way place to play, and we kids could occasionally leave our junk there without having to pick it up.

That verandah, we came to learn, had other exciting potentials that probably no one had yet comprehended.

# CHAPTER 29

# The Course of True Love

Like me, Dad went off to school every day. Because he taught college people, our house was often full of talk about classroom concerns and campus affairs. I really didn't know many of Dad's students, so I gave them very little thought. In fact, I didn't interest myself in these matters at all, until, one day, something very mysterious came up.

Occasionally some of the girls from the dorm would come over to visit my mother. One of them was Lonas Fleming. She was older than most of the girls. Indeed, she was quite elderly, almost like Mum. I suppose she may have been as much as thirty years old.

This time she came to stay with us for a whole weekend. She slept in Eileen's bed, and Eileen got a blanket on the floor. The visit didn't concern me much. Not that I didn't like her, but just nothing about her seemed all that important. My viewpoint, however, was about to change radically.

One of my Dad's students, Frank Burke, had been having a real problem. Also an older student, he had been noticing Lonas with far more interest than I had. The course of his love, however, proved to be beset with almost insurmountable difficulties.

As a super-conservative fundamentalist college, Australasian Missionary College, at that time, had regulations stipulating that Frank could not have a date with Lonas until he'd been "going with her" for three years. Inasmuch as he'd never seen her until he arrived on campus, any thought of fulfilling even that first obligation was manifestly impossible

Only by sheerest accident could he hope ever to sit with her at the dining table. In fact, table assignments were studiously made to avoid allowing any couples the joy of eating a meal together.

Being seen together anywhere on campus was, of course, absolutely out of the question. Certainly no student possessed his or her own car. Indeed the only transportation available was old Mrs. Andersen's rattletrap bus. A mere handful of faculty members owned cars, and they assuredly would never have promoted Frank's cause in any way.

On top of it all, exchanging letters smacked of subversive activity, and communications would probably be intercepted, worsening a couple's prospects still further.

About all Frank and Lonas had been able to accomplish thus far had been to look at one another meaningfully over great expanses of space. Wondering what his next step could legitimately be, Frank confided his problem to Dad. Always the champion of the under-dog, Dad promptly thought of a plan. "Saturday night you come down to my house for tea. You'll know what to do from there on."

Concurrently, Mum invited Lonas over for the entire weekend. At this point our parents took Eileen and me into the reckoning. Hindsight always being clearer than foresight, I know now that it would have been better if our parents had said nothing to us. We were instructed, however, that after tea Frank and Lonas would be sitting on the back porch by themselves. On no account should we open the door or even walk near it. Nor were we to look out of the kitchen windows.

I thought these admonitions very odd. Eileen, of course, looked to me for leadership, and I was perfectly willing to give it.

"What's going to happen to them out on the porch?" she asked. 'Why we couldn't watch?"

"We'll find out what

The Minchins revisited "The Laurels"—their home at Avondale College, New South Wales. Built by an American, the house was something of an anomaly among its Australian neighbors.

happens," I promised her. The answer to her second question, however, completely eluded me. Why couldn't we watch?

On the appointed evening affairs proceeded according to predictions. Eileen and I had some trouble getting through our food, being preoccupied with the thing that was going to happen on the back porch. I studied Frank and Lonas carefully. They ate heartily and seemed perfectly normal. Indeed, they seemed unusually cheerful.

Then, in precise fulfillment of the prophecy, Frank and Lonas left the table together and went out onto the screened verandah. Dad's foreknowledge amazed me. How did he know that that was exactly what they'd do?

They didn't turn on the light. I considered this a rather foolish negligence. How were they going to manage in the dark? Besides, whatever was going to happen might come upon them suddenly. Surely, they'd have been better off to have had the light on for protection. Any kid knew that you always left the bedroom door open a crack for the light, so that the bogey-man wouldn't get you.

Time passed by. Still no light and no sound. I began to be concerned. I decided to go to the kitchen to get a drink. Of course, Eileen was thirsty too. The light reflected in the windows, however, and I couldn't see anything on the porch. Without the kitchen light, though, we'd have seen nothing either.

We passed through the kitchen and went in to sit by the fireplace with Mum and Dad. We waited. After a while we trailed through the kitchen again for another drink. And another. And another. Still, we couldn't find out what was going on. I wondered if Frank and Lonas would ever come out. Maybe they'd already been seized and carried away. Who could tell?

After a while, Eileen and I couldn't hold any more water, so we stopped going through the kitchen. Neither Dad nor Mum seemed at all concerned. Dad busied himself with his papers. Mum, instead of washing up as she should have done, had left the dishes in the sink. She just sat there calmly darning socks by the fire in the living room.

When it became evident that Eileen and I weren't going to find out anything, we went to bed, waterlogged and much disgruntled.

A couple of years later I found out what really happened on Frank and

Lonas's first date, for that's what it was. The next morning a jubilant Frank came to thank Dad for his help. "We're engaged!" he exulted. "We decided to get it all fixed up last night because we didn't know when we'd get a chance to see each other again." Good on them!

Being engaged, naturally, did bring them a few dating privileges, such as they were. That meant, at least, that they could sit together with a dozen other couples in the public parlor in the girls' dormitory on a Saturday night. Officially, they were now "going together." As for sitting at the same table in the dining hall, well that was still the luck of the draw.

When I finally came to understand all of these fascinating circumstances, I wasn't surprised to learn later that the Frank Burkes had named their first two children after my father and my mother, respectively.

Two of Avondale's original buildings have been preserved in the drawings of M. Bruce Durant: The Girls Dormitory (Preston Hall) and Bethel Hall. *(Avondale College Centenary Print Collection, 1897-1987. Limited edition lithographic print. Used by permission.)*

# CHAPTER 30

# Towlers Bay and Other Diversions

Although we were separated by the seventy miles of railway line between Dora Creek and Wahroonga, it was perfectly predictable that our two families would spend holiday time together. The enormous zest we cousins had for being together made it obligatory for our parents to plan that way. To be sure, the four of them enjoyed time shared too. Those seventeen years' absence, after all, was a long time to make up.

Swimming was, and is, a national pastime in Australia. I'd swim with the kids in Dora Creek, because I never wanted to be left out. It paralyzed me, though, just to walk over the swing bridge to our swimming hole. Still worse, I hated the jellyfish, those massive orange, four-tentacled ones that lived in the Creek. I'd play around the edges, but only occasionally would I work up enough courage to run on the rope with the ring in the end. Then I'd swing out into the middle of the stream and drop into the dark creek water. Knowledge of the jelly fish down there utterly demoralized me.

My antipathy toward jellyfish also diminished much of my pleasure when our two families spent a week at The Entrance. Our parents being engrossed in church workers meetings, we children were free to create our own entertainment. Magnetically, the water and the boats drew us all down to the shore.

The Minchin Company usually presented a united front in the rather large group of children at loose ends there, looking for diversion. Occasionally, however, we drew the battle lines up with boys against girls. Or, again, the older against the younger. Or sometimes The Minchins against everyone else.

Whatever the current political climate, the weapons remained the same—jelly fish. At the opening of Lake Macquarie, The Entrance contained vast schools of white jellyfish, thick as sago pudding. The white moon discs contained little else than clear jelly with only the most minimal remains of brain and internal organs. Yet I hated to touch them.

My reticence made me exceedingly vulnerable in the great jellyfish fights that convened daily. Every morning began the same, with vigorous, beach-browned little kids wading among the boats gathering up jellyfish. When a jellyfish hit you, you first felt the smart of a high-velocity blob of jelly smacking your bare back or face. Then followed the irritation of jellyfish "chemicals," compounded with sunburn and sand.

In a matter of minutes, the banks of the lake were littered with broken chunks—with heaps—of dying jellyfish. The sun melted them rather quickly, of course, but it left the battlefield slick as a buttered griddle.

Somehow our arsenal never failed. The next morning there would be as many jellyfish as ever. The warfare continued. Contrary to the reasoning of some contemporary military strategists, if you have the striking power, you will use it. As long as the jellyfish held out, we'd fight.

The real beach holidays were the ones I enjoyed most. We went to Towlers Bay for our major mid-summer vacation, at Christmas time. A large, unspoiled inlet north of Sydney, it had summer cottages for rent, all decently set at widely spaced distances. For our crowd, Dad and Uncle Len found a long, rambling house with a spacious verandah across the front.

**Towlers Bay still maintains our dear little beach.**

Joy of joys, just below on the beach we had a walled-in swimming pool that filled and emptied with the tide. Although anything but scenic, the walls did keep out both sharks and jellyfish. There at the pool, day after day, we watched Dad and Uncle Len teaching Mum and Auntie May how to swim. Then-and for the next thirty-five years-they were always trying to teach them how to swim. Neither of them ever learned. At Towlers Bay we kids who lived totally amphibian lives simply couldn't understand, but we weren't surprised. Our mothers had to be too old—somewhere on their way to their forties.

Two rowboats came with the house. Indeed, no road existed, and the only way to reach the house was by boat from the far side of the bay. We rowed over to the village for groceries every couple of days. Such delicious privacy must have made our work-weary parents very happy. Busy as usual with our own creative projects, we children certainly didn't feel isolated.

Auntie Ruby and our older cousins came to be with us over Christmas. In their twenties, Jess and Verna could be a lot of fun. In general, however, they were too old to join in our really important affairs. Actually, we felt sorry for them, being so aged and not having much of anything left to look forward to.

In any case, a tremendous family experience happened in that beautiful place that summer. A chapter so spectacular that to this day the words "Towlers Bay" stand like a beacon shining across the years. One of the great milestones of our lives. Yet, how simple it all was. Just the perfect family holiday, that's all.

Down the middle of the main room ran a very long table. It seated us all at one time to eat the meals which the women served out of the smoky, pokey little kitchen. At night, after tea, we'd play "Up Jenkins Flop" at the same table and scream ourselves hoarse. The game was a loud version of "Ring-on-the-String" in which one team had to locate a shilling being passed among the members of the opposite side. Upon command, you had to slam your hands down on the table, hoping to conceal the sound of the coin—if you happened to have it.

Washing dishes for such a large household was officially the kids' task, at least part of the time. Fair enough. The moment we'd finished eating, however, we'd exchange a secret signal, and the six of us would rush, in a body, down to the boats. Then we'd row out into the almost-land-locked bay.

Mum wisely withheld Eileen from boat adventures unless an adult were along. For the rest of us, however, Kelvin was good enough. He'd already begun, in great earnest, his life-long love affair with boats. That summer he'd started building his first sailboat. For the holidays, he'd made a little toy boat for each of us girls to play with. Already a notable sailor, he created a very satisfying level of panic one morning by taking out one of the rowboats—minus the oars—powered only by a sail he'd made out of a blanket.

Sometimes we caught fish, a new experience for me. I didn't care for it much. Yvonne, for one at least, could bravely cut off their heads. Some members of the family ate them. I, somehow, couldn't quite make the right connection. The silvery fish cavorted so gracefully in the sun's light pools just off the white-sand beach. Eating them just didn't occur to me as something I wanted to do.

In our after-meals excursions, we'd drop anchor a couple of hundred yards offshore. By that time, our parents would have stopped their table talk and started thinking about cleaning up the kitchen. Where were the kids who were supposed to be doing the dishes?

The big rambling house where we lived for two weeks has burned to the ground. Only the fireplace and chimney remain.

We stayed safely at sea, communing among ourselves. We could see the adults along the railing of the verandah, gesticulating and calling to us. The message came through clearly enough. We understood exactly what they wanted. Kelvin knew just how far out we needed to take the boats so that we couldn't actually hear them.

"You know, we really ought to go back and do the dishes," Joan would say. "Don't you think we should go in?"

"Well, not necessarily," Kelvin would counter. "We can't hear what they're saying, can we? We might be going in for nothing."

"Yes," Yvonne and I would join in. "We don't really know what they want. They might all just be talking to each other."

So we'd stay out for hours, exploring the little coves, beaching our craft, climbing the rocks, romping on the white sand in the clean, eddying water, and basking in the sunshine. Just being innocent, contented children on an Australian summer's day!

Our parents were normally strict disciplinarians, but things were different at Towlers Bay. They really didn't enforce the business of cleaning up the kitchen. By common consent they just let childhood carry on a little while longer. I suppose they knew, as we all would later discover, that in the years to come there would be ample time and opportunity to wash dishes and make beds. But there would never be, for any of us, another Towlers Bay. Nor could there be.

Other, shorter holiday times usually took us to the local Sydney beaches. Perhaps to Bondi, or, better still, the ferry-ride out across the harbor to Manly Beach. Knowing that we had but a single day, we would give ourselves up wholly to beach madness.

Our parents would set themselves up on the sand. Dad and Uncle Len would

We loved the endless sand, sun, and surf at Manly, one of Sydney's best beaches.

walk, Mum would hunt for shells and Auntie would knit. We could never comprehend such a waste of a good beach. Why didn't they stay in the water all day as we did? It had to do with their advanced age, a thought that rather obsessed us. Sad, being too old to enjoy the treat they were giving us.

We'd spend hours in the water, never coming out once, unless the lifeguard rang the bell and shouted "Shark!" or Auntie called us to lunch. We'd dance in the waves in circles of ecstasy. Stride out to meet them. Dive into them. Let them twist and turn us inside out. They'd tie our legs in knots, smash us onto the bottom and choke us with sand until we were totally waterlogged.

Kelvin Minchin's passion for sailing boats never waned. He practiced medicine throughout his working years in the United States. In retirement, however, he returned to New Zealand to live within reach of Auckland, the sailing capital of the world.

All of our beach days ended the same way. Going home on the train, almost too tired to climb up into the carriage. Burned scarlet, our skins stretched over our weary bones like old, cracked leather underwear. When we'd get home, we'd have the anointing, with every tortured, scorched little body lined up to have soothing lotion applied to the hurts. Then, a few grumbles and maybe some tears, and away to bed. We'd be so shaken up that our beds seemed to rock, and we'd ride the waves all night.

At the very next opportunity, we'd be off again. No memory of the pain, only exhilaration for spending another day in the surf. All of those many decades ago we knew that our sunburns were painful but we always recovered. No one had told us yet that they could be deadly.

Our holiday cycles taught us, if nothing else, the reality of that hope which "springs eternal" in us all. Even as our raging sunburns healed and as we spent easy, idle hours peeling layers of skin off one another's backs, so exuberance and optimism welled

The family's love of the sea has historic roots. The *Caroline* brought James Minchin and his family from England to the Swan River Colony, Western Australia, in 1829. *(By Eileen Minchin-Davis)*

up within us once more.

Anything that teaches that every day is a new beginning can't be all bad, no matter how painful.

A group of young men walked discreetly by the front door of the girl's dormitory (Preston Hall) at Avondale College in 1941. They knew that their chances of sitting with a girlfriend in the dining room in the basement were about as bleak as qualifying for a communal "group date" in the parlor, just inside the front door.

# CHAPTER 31

# On My Own

When school reopened in February, 1943, I entered Grade 7 at the Avondale Central School. Although still shy and uncertain, I began to find a niche for myself. I had to do it without the support of the cousins. To be sure, I'd much rather have been in school back in Wahroonga, but now I had to carve out my identity alone. The constant, gnawing awareness of being a foreign misfit slowly began to fade. For a thirteen-year-old it had been an agonizing trial.

Every day after classes I retraced the half-mile I'd walked to school in the morning. Mid-way home I'd passed the college dairy. When I'd dumped my books and lunch box at home, I took the "billy" (Australian, "little pail") and returned to the dairy for the day's supply of milk.

Walking that road alone lacked the stimulus that walking with my compatriots in Wahroonga always had. Through natural processes, I stopped the stone-kicking business. Even though my shoes were certainly the better for it, my heart always reached out after those cousins I'd left behind in Wahroonga.

Then things took a turn for the better. Suddenly, for the first time, I tasted the intoxication of making top grades. This thrust me into lively competition with Jill, the girl who'd been topping the class for several years. Naturally, I appeared on the scene as some kind of imposter. I relished this heady new experience and couldn't think of giving it up.

"My father's going to give me a shilling every time I get the top grade." Jill accosted me at recess, eyeing me smugly as she tossed her blond curls and twisted the toe of her shoe into the gravel.

Because I'd never before been a candidate for such awards, I hadn't even considered the monetary advantages inherent in good performance. Therefore, I made a point of informing Dad about Jill's arrangement with her father. My allowance being but sixpence a week, I saw here the possibility of more financial security.

Dad, dear wise father that he was, just looked down at me for a long time. "Well, Dottie, it's all right, I guess, but I don't think that we can do that."

Later on, I realized that there simply weren't enough shillings to be spent in that fashion. More important, however, Dad didn't want me to develop an exploitative, commercial mentality that would become troublesome later.

Instead, he just put his arm around me and said, "Just remember that every time you get a good grade your old Dad knows that you can do good work. Remember too that he'll be so proud of you, he'll probably bust all his buttons off!"

Believe it or not, that simple faith and commitment from my father—nothing more—ultimately carried me out into the far reaches of higher education and scholarship.

I realize now that the young teachers at Avondale Central School needed all their strength and ingenuity just to survive their jobs. As a practice field for the teacher-training department at the college, our school entertained a procession of earnest, would-be teachers. We tested them, baited them, and made their lives as wretched as they would permit us to do. Having already experienced student teachers in Wahroonga, I knew the rules of the game.

I found in my classroom at Avondale, however, that the kids employed some creative techniques I'd never seen before. Wally Dawson proved to be one of the most talented in this line.

Mr. Bill Driscoll had lived through his college apprenticeship, and this job was his first year on regular staff as homeroom teacher for the Grade 8 class. For the first few weeks of school he taught us Latin.

One morning, he laboriously copied a large declension of verbs on the blackboard. "Dorso!" He addressed Wally by his familiar schoolyard title. "Tell me what the stem of this is." He pointed to a word near the top of the list.

Being absorbed in some nefarious private enterprise behind the lid of his desk, Dorso didn't have the faintest idea what the question pertained to. Never one to be depressed, however, he looked up at Mr. Driscoll from under his unruly shock of platinum blond hair. The very freckles on his nose seemed to quiver in his sudden concern and commitment. "Do you mean the stem of a . . . a flower, sir?" He smiled up at the teacher in cheerful but faked innocence.

Electric silence swept through the room. In our eagerness to know what would happen next, we could hardly breathe. Had he been a more experienced teacher, Mr. Driscoll would have found a way to avoid a confrontation. As we've already observed, however, he was very young.

I watched a flush of red creep up above Bill Driscoll's striped, starched shirt collar. It suffused his face, right up into his curly blond hair. "Dorso! Stand up." The teacher drew himself up tall beside the front desk. "Come here!"

Wally went forward, stooped in apparent contrition. We all knew what Mr. Driscoll couldn't know, that Dorso's humility was nothing but a sham. "Go to my classroom and bring me a cane." He kept a selection of canes of varying weights and lengths in a wastebasket by his desk over in the Grade 8 classroom. While Dorso was gone—a considerable time—Mr. Driscoll tried to keep the Latin class going but with only moderate success.

Presently the condemned one returned bearing a small, splintered piece of bamboo. The teacher ignored our smothered snickers of amusement. The whole affair was turning out to be fun!

Sensing by now that he needed some privacy, Mr. Driscoll led Wally into a very small, crowded broom closet that opened off the classroom. We all knew, of course, that there wouldn't be room to swing a cane properly in that tiny space.

Committed to what he'd begun, however, Driscoll lashed Dorso as soundly as he could. We could hear the thrashing against the door. In due course, the two emerged, Wally first, grinning affably. Obviously the punishment hadn't really touched him anywhere, body, mind or spirit. Behind him came the teacher bearing the straw-like shreds of what had once been his instrument of discipline.

That day we found out how far we could get Mr. Driscoll to go. While he went on to become an educator of some considerable stature in later years, I like to think that those irritating things we did to him in the old Central

School classroom may have contributed something to the consolidating of his fine character.

Robert Parr came into our lives a little late, having just been "de-mobbed" out of the Army. Perhaps the fact that the first time we saw him he was still in his military uniform had something to do with the power he had over us. For the first time in my life I noticed what a good-looking man could be like. The wavy dark hair, the infectious smile, the sense of humor, and all of the rest. I enslaved myself to him when he took over the Latin class. I made 98% on the first test.

For the first time in my life, I think, I stopped to consider seriously the mystery of male attraction. Of course, I still didn't care about boys as such, most of whom seemed to be on the order of Wally Dawson. Still, the first vague stirrings of interest in a grown-up, self-possessed, interesting man now moved within me.

On sunny spring days Mr. Parr sometimes took us out into the school-yard where we sat on logs under the ti-trees. Very courageous of him, for the leaves hid big exotic lizards and beetles. The smell of the fragrant bush-land threatened to draw us away from books. He, however, held everything together and learning Latin remained a viable project out there.

Avondale College Chapel *(used by permission, M. Bruce Durrant).*

I cannot remember precisely the nature of the misdemeanor that brought me to detention one day after school. Probably talking too much. Certainly it wasn't anything as original as what Dorso went to detention for.

That afternoon, unhappily, I found Mr. Parr to be the supervisor of my punishment session. I slid into one of the back desks, feeling like something dark and slimy that lives under a rock. I started writing my 500 lines that, hopefully, would condition me never to speak aloud in the classroom again.

When finished, I stumbled blindly to the front and gave him my sheaf of papers. Mr. Parr didn't betray unusual horror at my crime. He just remarked, with a twinkle in his eye, "But you were a bit of a chump, weren't you?"

I agreed wholeheartedly. I had been a chump. Or anything else that he might have cared to call me that day.

# CHAPTER 32

# Baby Brother

Having grown up in a world of both innocence and ignorance, I'd arrived at the age of twelve still without any very clear understanding of matters relating to babies and pregnancy.

When Mum was expecting her third child, I didn't even see anything peculiar about Miss Walker's counsel from upstairs, "Now you must be very careful, Mrs. Minchin. The baby might get out of place and rupture your jugular vein!"

Mum remembered my disappointment at the birth of Eileen when I had been wholly excluded from the whole episode. So this time she shared the event with me almost from the start. I immediately felt very responsible.

The family was obviously over-stocked with girls already, so we generally assumed that this would be a baby brother. It hardly occurred to me that there could be any other option. The cousins felt the same, especially Kelvin.

A few years earlier he'd gloomily considered the arrival of his twin sisters. "All these girls!" he muttered. "And Mummy's a girl, and the cat's a girl, and the cow's a girl and the chooks (chickens) are girls, and ... " His voice trailed off plaintively as he remembered how hard he'd prayed for a baby brother. "But," he went on, trying to rationalize the misfortune, "I guess God just didn't have a

The old Sydney Sanitarium was a long-time landmark in Wahroonga, NSW, Australia. Here Baby Keith Minchin lived his few hours of life.

**Physicians and nursing staff gathered on the verandahs of the old Sanitarium. What is left of the original building is now hidden within ultra-modern Sydney Adventist Hospital.**

little boy to send, so He gave us two girls to make up for it."

No question about it. This baby ought to be a boy. We simply didn't need another girl. Preparations for the coming of the baby evolved into a major family project. While Eileen still preferred playing with our big Persian cat Timbo, even she sometimes got caught up in the excitement. I helped Mum hem the big flannel nappies (diapers). I spent a long time studying the intricate pattern of the blue crib cover that Lil Abbott had knitted for my little brother. The growing collection of woolly baby things enthralled me.

Then suddenly, one early mid-winter morning in late July, Dad took Mum to the hospital. I knew the right day hadn't come yet, but I was still too inexperienced to understand any of the hazards or complications connected with having babies.

"Auntie Ruby will look after you while we're gone." Dad climbed into the principal's car beside Mum for the seventy-mile trip down to Sydney Sanitarium. "Be a good big sister to Eileen."

In a few minutes Auntie Ruby came to get us. We packed up our little travel bags, put Timbo in a box and walked the familiar woodsy path over to Amen Gate and Auntie's house. The prospect of spending some days there almost made me forget that my parents' departure had been anxious and in haste.

From Auntie's house to Avondale Central School was only an easy skip-and-a-hop through the bush along another winding path. The next day I came bounding home for lunch at the noon hour. I just had to announce how well I'd played quoits at recess and how one of the big ninth-grade girls had chosen me to be on her team.

Instead, Auntie Ruby stood in the doorway, arms akimbo, smiling. "You have a baby brother!" she said, giving me a hug. "They've named him Keith Rowland."

So it had happened! It had really happened! I sat down on the back steps, to steady myself and to let the idea sink in. A real little boy had come to live with us. Now we'd be Eight Little Australians. I just let the great wave of happiness sweep over me.

Then, awash with joy, I siphoned off my bean soup, grabbed my peanut butter-and-banana sandwich, and shot through the back door again. I had to get back to school to tell all the kids about Keith. I raced through the melon patch and flew low down the bush track. Even when a big brown-and-yellow snake slithered across the path, I cleared him in a single leap.

My momentum carried me back into the school yard before most of the kids had eaten halfway through their lunches. As far as I was concerned, there'd never been another baby born in all of the world. At least, not one like this one.

As usual, my school mates were happy enough to hear any new thing, and I got a lot of attention from bearing these glad tidings. Even the teachers were interested in my news, in a polite sort of way.

After school I couldn't wait to get back to Auntie and hear more of the wonder that had come to us. I seemed to be running a foot above the ground as I galloped back through the woods.

When I crashed into the kitchen, I knew that something had

In Avondale's pioneer cemetery, Gerald and Leona Minchin stood by the grave of their baby son, Keith.

**The laughter of kookaburras still begins and ends the days around Cooranbong.**

changed. Something intangible in the house stopped me cold. Eileen sat under the dining table with her doll and her ginger teddy bear, but Auntie Ruby stood very still, just looking at me. She seemed very tired.

Without a word she put her arms around me and led me into her bedroom—her lovely quiet place where the afternoon sun filtered through the lace curtains and picked out patterns on her rose satin comforter. We sat down together on the bed.

"My dear little Dottie!" She held me tight and rested my head on her shoulder. "Baby Brother died this afternoon."

I sat up and stared at her. I couldn't understand anything of her meaning. The only things I knew that had died were bugs, mice, and squashed things beside the road. Once I'd watched the *kabun* (gardener) kill a snake in our yard in Singapore. But people? And never, surely never, a new baby brother!

Finally I knew. I had to know, and, at last, the tears came. Auntie Ruby talked about heaven and how such a terrible thing could happen in our family. She explained how Jesus loves us more than ever when terrible things like this happen. She held me, and we cried together for a long time—until the sun dropped into the bush trees and the shadows turned the rosy room to gray.

Eileen didn't go to the funeral. She was just too small to understand what had happened. Neither did Mum go, for she was very, very sick in the hospital, struggling with toxemia.

I went to Avondale Cemetery, along with the friends and the neighbors. I listened to the kookaburras in the gum trees laughing at us. The white casket was so tiny. Inside I saw Keith, my brother. He was so very little and so very white, but he was perfect in his white silk dress with a white rose in his baby hands.

I stood in the rain between Auntie Ruby and my Dad. He had the collar of his overcoat pulled up around his ears. I'd never seen my father cry before. Then, amid the rain and the tears, Mr. Borringer set the little coffin down into the grave. He covered it up, and we all went home.

The previous day, down in Sydney, my five cousins had all been excused from school so that they could go up to the hospital and see the baby before he was put into his casket.

Now we all groped our way through the experience. We had planned so much for little Keith. He was going to be that all important little boy for us girls to fuss over. Kelvin was going to make him a wooden boat. Eileen was going to be there to play with him while the rest of us were away at school.

Little Brother came, and he went. We never even heard him cry.

Yet he changed us all. Afterwards we became different, more grown-up somehow. For the first time we children faced the fact that death must always be part of life. We learned the lesson well, and not one of us would ever forget.

# CHAPTER 33

# Our Short New Zealand Interlude

The end of our first year in Avondale now approached. With graduation time coming on, we all got tuned in to diplomas and such.

Never one to be left out of anything, Eileen suddenly became concerned about where she was going to fit into the forthcoming academic festival. At bedtime one night she asked in a wistful, small voice, "But, Daddy, when am I going to get my QLE?"

The four-year-old assumed that any combination of letters could make up an academic degree. Dad had to suppress his smile, however, for the little person in the horsy pajamas was in dead earnest. "Um. QLE?" he mused. Always quick with repartee, he replied, "Why, yes. I believe that stands for "Quick, Look at Eileen." He kissed the little candidate goodnight. "I think we can give you that degree tomorrow."

Sure enough, next morning, Eileen found beside her plate at breakfast a fully accredited diploma. Tied with a ribbon and complete with seal, the scroll granted her all of the rights and privileges of the QLE degree. It had been duly signed by one, "Professor Puffstuff."

When graduation day did come, no senior walked the center aisle of old Avondale chapel with a greater sense of accomplishment than did the holder of the QLE degree, trailing behind the procession with her mother, document in hand. As the academic dean, of course, Dad had every legal right to confer this honor upon his younger daughter! No question.

After many weeks of illness, Mum had just begun to seem normal again. I fondly anticipated years and years ahead to enjoy Australia, the cousins, and my new school friends. With spring coming on, we were supposed to be planning another Towlers Bay holiday.

Instead, something was amiss. Heart-breakingly so. Our first year at Avondale was also to be our last. We were to move to New Zealand where Dad would teach at New Zealand Missionary College near Palmerston North.

Much later I learned that the problem grew out of a complex political situation. Someone wanted Dad's job, and he got it. Years down the road, I believe that some fences got mended, at least a little. Although I never wanted to know all of the details, I do know that Dad's inability to work in his beloved homeland was one of the most devastating disappointments he ever endured. Not that it ruined his career. No. But he carried the pain of that event for the rest of his life.

I dreaded the thought of another move with all of its attendant adjustments. Now to face yet another wilderness of loneliness, to break into another new school, to be the odd new kid again. My loyalties ran deep, but not less so than my father's. So with a notable lack of enthusiasm we packed up for New Zealand. To top it all off, none of us had recovered from losing Baby Brother such a short time before.

Down in Sydney Harbor the reality of separation hit us all. I believe no ship ever sailed out of Sydney Heads carrying more heartbreak and tears than did ours. The grief was nonetheless real, just because it belonged to children. Even Eileen joined in stormy weeping for "mine Twinnies."

Of course, we'd always write letters. In our teen years we'd share homes and good times in both Old England and New England. Some of us would live together all the way through college, and beyond. The vision of those happy days still to come completely eluded us that sad spring morning in November, 1942.

We arrived in Wellington's hill-ringed harbor three days later, little mended from our sorrows. We disembarked into winds that almost lifted us up and blew us back out to sea again.

The train journey north to the college took us through some fabulously lovely countryside, but I know this only because of a much later visit. At the time, the landscape of heaven itself would scarcely have assuaged my grief in leaving my life behind in Australia.

The college lay in the valley of the Manawatu River, completely surrounded by paddocks (fields) full of grazing sheep. The village of Longburn stood at the end of the college road, on the main route to Palmerston. The school itself consisted primarily of a single building. The large central portion contained offices, classrooms and the dining room, while the boys' dormitory occupied the left wing and the girls' the right.

The house allotted to us was not ready yet, so we ended up living for six weeks in a couple of rooms in the boys' end of the school building. I rather enjoyed the social life, eating with the students in the dining hall and working at my very first job.

In fact, it didn't even seem a half bad place to be for Christmas. The matron, Marian Thompson, made an inexhaustible supply of steamed plum puddings, with threepences and sixpences concealed in them. Also, a great kettle of custard to go with them. The puddings, eaten on top of a full Christmas dinner, challenged the best we had to give.

One lanky, hardy fellow, Leon Wolff, ate seven helpings of pudding, in quest of silver coins. For all that, he still found nothing. The next morning, we learned, Nurse Thrift had to wait on him, for he was violently ill all night.

I, on the other hand, found a sixpence and two threepences—a whole shilling—in my first serving of pudding. Not bad, considering that I earned half that, a mere six-pence an hour, in my job on the school farm.

Through the rest of summer vacation I picked peas in the college garden and ironed shirts in the college laundry. When I landed a place in the basket factory, I realized that I'd become elite, an aristocrat on the labor scene. For a thirteen-year-old it was a fair responsibility. Too naive to realize how little sixpence was, I simply took unadulterated pride in now earning some of my own way through school.

One weekend a Jewish businessman and his family, refugees from Czechoslovakia, came to spend the weekend at the college. Not wanting to embarrass him, our mothers explained that on Friday night the visitors would be lighting some candles and having special prayers. Also that the father would be wearing a funny little hat but that we were, on no account, to stare at it or say anything about it.

We had just enough information to make us curious about the Friday night ceremonies. In due course, the family arrived and was escorted into the dining room as guests of honor. The sun was setting, and we knew the candles would be lit.

Part of the ceremony, however, was missing! Eileen voiced the thoughts of a great many people when she inquired loudly, "But, Mummy!" Her voice quavered with disappointment, but it carried perfectly, clear back into the kitchen. "Why isn't the man wearing his funny hat?"

The good man had left off his *yarmulke* (cap). Some of us saw that when the flutter had subsided, the rabbi furtively pulled it out of his pocket and set it on the back of his head. Surely, there's something to be said for leaving well enough alone, especially where kids are concerned. A few days later, I felt my first earthquake. Quite a sharp one that tended to make me forget the oddities of the Jewish rabbi's Friday night practices.

On a cool spring day in Longburn, students and staff mingle in front of the "All-in-One" building of New Zealand Missionary College (1942). The Minchins spent one school year there en route back to America.

The people at NZMC made us very welcome but were rather surprised to see us. Dad's teaching load was something of a mixed bag. He had little subject matter for which he'd had any training. From the start, I guess everyone knew that our "New Zealand Interlude" would be a short one. In fact, most of our boxes remained in the spare bedroom, unopened.

As always we were poor. Finding ways to economize and cut corners had been the story of Mum's life. Among her other thrifty endeavors, she decided to fit out Dad, Eileen and me in flour-sack pajamas. The flour sacks cost almost nothing and lasted for years. Indeed, they could be virtually indestructible. She always trimmed the garments with colorful scraps of other cloth, intending thereby to distract our attention from the hard stiffness of the fabric. When new, the flour-sack pajamas were rather like going to sleep wrapped in a ship's sail.

That winter Mum decided, since I was "still growing," to model my lingerie off Dad's pattern. Never patient to have garments tried out on me, however, I didn't stop for a fitting until my pajamas neared completion.

Then, one night, standing in front of our tiny coal fireplace, I submitted to my first trial. Having renounced fashion and vanity long before, I put the pajamas on with an elaborate air of boredom.

Once into them, however, I became alarmed. Four-inch hems and a great bulk around the middle! When I pulled the waistband up to my armpits, the crotch still hung below my knees. The legs trailed out at least six inches beyond my feet. The jacket hit me at mid-calf, and my hands fell six or eight inches short of the ends of the sleeves. Would I ever find my way out alive? The grotesqueness of the sight startled even Dad. "Jumping gingers!" he exclaimed. "What's that?"

What indeed? A veritable clown suit! We all had a good laugh over it. Poor Mum, of course, made alterations. Finally, it began to dawn on me that maybe it did matter what clothes I wore. At least, I think I began to care a little bit.

Although I didn't know it at the time, the transfer to New Zealand had begun to mark the end of an era. I suddenly had to make my way among students much older than I. Instinctively I tried to measure up. In all the traveling about I had, without realizing it, shaved off a few months here and there. Now, at least two years too soon, I already stood on the threshold of Grade 9.

My closest friend, Beryl Bade, came down from Palmerston every day, but even she was two years older than I. All of the girls in the Basket Factory, I discovered, lived seriously adult lives. The supervisor, Edna Hambling, was even engaged to be married! Never in my life had I been close to someone who was planning to do that!

So, day by day, I sat at my bench weaving baskets, the wet canes rubbing my fingers raw. I listened intently all the while to the big-girl conversation that swirled around me. The fact that they treated me as an equal wrought some mighty changes in me. Marion, Fay, Pearl, Joan, Gladys and the others made me a friend and didn't seem to find me silly at all!

Very soon now the door would be closing on my childhood. I could hardly see that far ahead, though. Not yet.

Our house, half a mile down the Longburn road was just a little square box. It looked out on the sheep paddocks on three sides and a slaughterhouse on the far side of the fields. I loved the sheep, and the squeals and cries of the doomed animals

The Longburn house (which never got "unpacked") remains amid the sheep paddocks. Although its color changes from time to time, the neighborhood has not.

chilled my bone marrow. I hated what was going on over there, especially after Peter came into our lives.

We arrived home one day to find a newborn lamb lying in the wash-shed, too weak to stand up. The farm manager gave us a hard black nipple which we fastened to a large ginger-beer bottle. Eileen and I took turns feeding Peter. He grew larger by the hour, it seemed. We'd often go outside to find Eileen lying flat on her back where Peter had bowled her over while he stood above her sucking on his bottle that she still held in her hands.

Dorothy and Eileen with their beloved lamb, Peter, who believed that he was a dog.

She never cried because of his rough games.

Dad made a small attempt at a garden again. Peter broke down the fence and harvested all of the spinach and Swiss chard while we were at church one day. Although Eileen and I thought that the lamb had rendered a fine public service, our parents didn't share our view.

Whoever invented the myth about "gentle as a lamb" simply didn't have all of the facts. By the time we left Longburn Peter was a strapping young ram with a glorious thick fleece. He thought he was a dog, and we loved him very much. The man we finally gave him to promised that never, under any circumstances, would he send Peter to the slaughterhouse. I still like to imagine, after all of these years, that he kept his word.

During the whole school year we never really settled in our house. Dad's work situation remained unchanged. World War II still raged on. My American Grandma was sick. Dad wanted to begin graduate studies. Yes, there were good and sufficient reasons for moving back to the United States. Having lost Australia and being unable to remember much of significance about America, I didn't care one way or another what we did. One place seemed as good as another. Somewhere down the line I might turn out to be an American, after all.

New Zealand, thus, became a strange, sad mixture in my mind. Lovely country! From our front door we could see the volcano Ruapehu steaming to the northwest! We could walk down through the meadows to watch the eels in the river and enjoy the velvet, green Manawatu Hills beyond.

I never felt settled. Always a pilgrim, just passing through. The house never seemed warm. I was, in fact, in the middle of a very unsettling transition time for our family. I would end up going to seven different schools in seven countries in seven consecutive years. It seemed that I always had to be in the middle of "starting new."

Near the end of the school year, a new sorrow entered my life. The packing had started again. We didn't know exactly when we could leave because we would have to find passage on a ship in a military convoy. Every day Mum diligently did some sorting. I came home one evening to find that my beloved Gold Teddy Bear had been burned at the stake that morning. He

# CHAPTER 34

# Another Door Opens, Creaking

Back to America where I'd begun! But it was never a simple matter of geography. No, it was a great deal more than that. It took me more than a year to discover even a few of the far reaching implications of our move. I had no idea what I was up against.

On Wednesday night, February 23, 1944, we arrived in San Pedro, Port of Los Angeles. I stood on the deck watching the soldiers stream off down the gangplanks. Several big, shiny cars had been parked on the dock. Mingled in were military police, sirens, flashing spotlights, and peculiar, drawly speech on all sides. So this was America! I felt as strange there as a nomad from the steppes of Central Asia.

Spending the summer with my mother's family hid my real problems from me. Just before he returned to Borneo, Uncle Gus and Auntie Norma Youngberg had bought a house on the edge of La Sierra College, Riverside, California. Auntie Norma was to get the family sorted out and then follow him back to the Far East.

Grandpa Rhoads' health problems had necessitated moving from Iowa to a warmer, drier climate. So he and Grandma were to keep the house while the Youngberg kids went to school. The plan had been only partially successful. The war had totaled out everything. Uncle Gus had been imprisoned in a concentration camp in Kuching, Sarawak. In fact, at this time, he was already dead, but no one knew it yet.

Grandpa and Grandma had been told little of our plan to return to the United States. Our departure from New Zealand and even the journey itself had been too uncertain. A chronic worrier, Grandma didn't need anything more to upset her. So we reached the big sprawling house on Raley Drive that

Friday morning without their knowing that Dad was doing anything other than still working at NZMC.

"I have a surprise for you." Auntie Norma announced. "You need to sit down here on the couch before I bring it in."

Six-year-old Eileen, whom they'd never seen, headed the procession. I came next, followed by Mum and Dad. Great excitement, tears, laughter and general uproar.

Other changes had come about among my Youngberg cousins. At ten years old, Ben had become a surprisingly skilled young naturalist and taxidermist. Intelligent, yes, but he loyally defended the daily blunders of his big brown hound, Blitz, an excessively stupid dog. Jimmy had turned into a tall, handsome teenager who took care of the chickens, milked Grandpa's cow, Brindle, and worked hot days in the boysenberry patch. About to enter college, Madge was on the point of marrying. It was Milton Longway though, not William of Orange after all.

Meanwhile, Grandpa had decided to build a little one-bedroom home for himself and Grandma, right next to the big Youngberg house. After a lifetime of frugality, he wasn't about to be reckless now. Oh, no! So he collected hundreds of tough, wooden ammunition boxes from March Air Force Base, nearby. No throwing away money on a bulldozer either. He and we grandchildren dug the basement out with shovels. We worked hard and responsibly, stopping only occasionally to have clod fights.

When people passed on the road and saw this seventy-two-year-old man stacking the ammunition boxes for walls, they'd wonder what he was doing. "Well," he liked to say, "they told me I was going to die

The family crossed the war-ravaged Pacific in convoy, aboard the troop transport ship, *Mariposa* (1944). The voyage from Wellington, New Zealand to San Pedro (Los Angeles), Southern California, took almost a month.

and sent me out to California." He'd pull his big red handkerchief out of his overalls pocket and wipe his face. "So I've waited a while for the undertaker, but since he's not coming yet, I'm building me a house."

Aunt Blanche had also joined the little family compound, Uncle John Spriggs having died long ago. Grandpa built a little apartment for her in the basement of his box-house so she could move out of her trailer.

Well, that was the way of Grandpa. On his eighty-fourth birthday he'd be climbing the Washington Monument. At ninety he'd be keeping the garden at Mum's and Dad's place in Massachusetts. He'd live, in fact, to be almost 100. Doctors do make mistakes.

Spending that summer in the bosom of the family provided a buffer zone for my re-entry into American life. Since Madge was in summer school, I also picked up a summer course that would qualify me to enter Grade 10 in the autumn.

Madge and I slept on the roof of the porch most of the summer, bundled up in blankets against the cool, desert nights. We lay in the moonlight looking up to the boulder-strewn hills silhouetted against the southern sky. Sometimes we could see the coyotes that bayed at the moon. We spent long evenings up there reading the novels of Jane Austen and Charles Dickens, by flashlight.

Once again, I was under the spell of Madge, but things had changed. By now ghost stories and horror tales were irrelevant. We talked about teenage concerns. At thirteen I was on the low end, and at almost twenty she was a woman. As always she bent my life into shape, and I had implicit faith in her wisdom. I only wished that she'd had time to accomplish more improvements on me.

I had submitted to what was to be my last pumpkin-bowl haircut just before we left New Zealand. Within six weeks I'd recovered from the worst of that scalping. So Madge set up my first beauty salon appointment and took me to get a permanent wave. Then she spent an evening inducting me into the mysteries of hair setting. The whole performance gave me a rather new view of myself. To my surprise, some of what I now saw I liked—when I happened to look in the mirror. That was still something I didn't do often.

Dad had decided to start graduate studies in Washington, D.C. So, at the end of the summer, we made the long trans-continental train journey. A leisurely four days to put us in touch again with the Big Country to which we'd chosen to return.

Upon our arrival, a great many things happened in a hurry. The humid summer heat stifled us in the attic apartment we rented on Flower Avenue. Mum landed an office job, Dad began to study for his MA degree in church history, and Eileen went into Grade 1. I entered Grade 10 at Takoma Academy. We'd never lived this way before, with all of us going out to work every day. The effects of the change could be upsetting.

For the school year (1944-1945) the Gerald Minchin family lived in the attic apartment of the M.E. Olson house on Flower Avenue, Takoma Park, Maryland. Extremes of heat and cold up there were insufferable, but since everyone was either in school or at work, we managed to be absent from home many hours of the day. Sometimes we remembered—with nostalgia—our airy home on the equator in Singapore.

My parents knew a few people in the city, but I didn't know one living creature. This knowledge chilled my innermost soul. I'd always made friends before, but in some way that I couldn't figure out, all of this was different. My school was full of handsome, debonair boys and flirty girls. Obviously they were made for one another. I looked at the girls carefully. Yes, thanks to Madge, my hair was all right. My clothes certainly weren't. I didn't know why, but the kids all seemed about eight years older than I. Somehow there still hung about me the shyness, the naiveté, and the ignorance of being a child!

Sheer stockings hadn't been a big deal in California, but I could see that they were in Washington. So Mum got me some, along with the necessary equipment for holding them up. The latter garment I despised, having never fully recovered from the harness-business back in Kansas City, I suppose.

My difficulty went deeper. Having been together in school for ten years, these kids formed a solid social block that seemed to have no room for even one more person. Especially not one with an odd semi-British accent and in short socks.

On top of that, I found that every girl in Grade 10 had a boyfriend. They thought of nothing but dates and the clothes that would be worn on those dates. I had never yet given these matters any thought. How does one find a boyfriend out of nowhere? Besides, once found, what would one do with him? I hadn't the least idea.

Like a drowning swimmer, going down for the third time, I struggled in this sea of sophistication. I thought a lot about Australia and my cousins. I wished Dad and Mum had just left me there. I wished the Japanese had sunk our ship to the bottom of the Pacific. I wished … I wished …

For consolation I turned to my old trusty friends, books. I liked my French teacher, Miss Esther Brucks. I studied and soared to the top of French II. I liked English and became an exhibition piece in Mrs. Plymire's English II class. I didn't like geometry, but with the help of Mr. Andross I survived. I took typing and worked up to the second highest speed in the bunch. I loved music, and I slaved in Miss,Winnifred Bane's music class. Dad rented an instrument for me, and I joined the band where I blew a solid second-chair clarinet. In my spare time I checked books out of Dad's graduate library. My interests that year ranged from finishing the rest of Dickens' novels as well as those of Sir Walter Scott. Also, Egyptian archeology. When I could, I'd take the streetcar to downtown Washington and hang out with the mummies at the Smithsonian Institution.

Gerald Minchin graduated with his M.A. in Church History in 1945. That happy event left the family free to move to their next home. This time it would be Canada.

Weekends I cleaned house for two aristocratic ladies near our apartment. With the few dollars I earned there, I began to think about clothes and high-heeled shoes. At five-foot-nine inches I didn't need heels, but I studied my environment and concluded that they were essential. At the same time, the boys I saw around seemed no more than five-foot-two. So what was the use? I felt awkward. Absolutely grotesque.

In despair, I'd go back to my books. All these years, and I still hadn't become a fairy-tale princess, even though I had managed to curl my hair. My fourteenth birthday passed, and no one outside of our attic apartment knew that it had happened.

Words can hardly describe the disaster that was that first year back in America. If I had even one friend, I don't know who it was. The teachers all regarded me with great favor, but that really didn't help much. In a way, it was a handicap. The thing I wanted most was to get through to the kids. For compensation, I had to retreat into ancient and medieval times.

I wrote letters to Australia. I wondered where we'd move to next.

Dorothy, Eileen, and their mother stand precisely and symbolically on the U.S.-Canadian International Border at Niagara Falls.

Finally the year ended. I cleaned out my locker and without one backward glance left Takoma Academy. Dad graduated with his MA degree, and we packed up to move to Canadian Union College. I'd formulated no opinions about the next school I'd go to. I didn't care where it was, so long as it wasn't in Washington.

Some subtle, undefined miracle, however, had begun during that whole miserable year. My Grade 11 experience turned out to be something entirely different. Suddenly I had plenty of friends. I also, had a couple of those very close, committed-for-a-lifetime friends that every girl needs. Even a few boys—great big, good-looking boys—sometimes found me interesting.

Life was full, fun, and wonderful. I almost fainted in the shock of it all. I know now that I had to spend that whole Washington year just learning to cross a busy and dangerous street.

At first, childhood is a warm cozy house. Then, as we grow older, we begin looking out of the windows and wondering about the world that's passing by on the street outside. After a while, our place seems too small. So we stand in the doorway, curious about all that traffic out there.

Across the street we see another house, hidden by trees. We think we'd like to go over to it. The garden looks beautiful. Many visitors come and go. It's time to move.

That's the way it was for me. I gently closed the door of my little house behind me. I crossed the street, picking my way through the traffic. Cautiously I walked up the driveway. I found it a very big house, for life itself is very large. I opened the door and stepped inside.

The first house we lived in at Canadian Union College was known as the "Union House" (long since demolished). We faced a whole new way of life and new friends, all under a sunny but unrelenting cover of snow.

Still, that little house back across the street will always be there. No kind of urban planning can ever tear it down. I know that I can never return to it. I can live in it again only by remodeling it in paper and announcing "Open House!"

I realize now that my Paper House is, in many ways, the most valuable piece of real estate I'll ever own!

# Part IV

# The Family Tree

# The Minchin Family Tree*

*See Dorothy Minchin-Comm, *The Book Minchin: A Family for All Seasons* (Trafford, 2006).

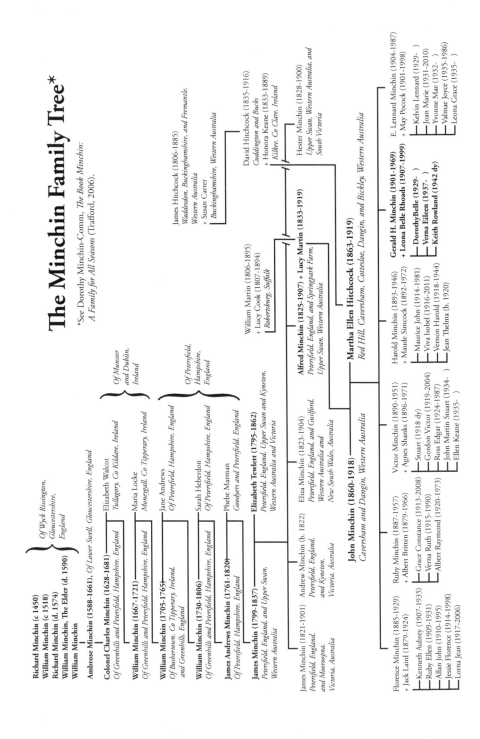

# The Rhoads Family Tree

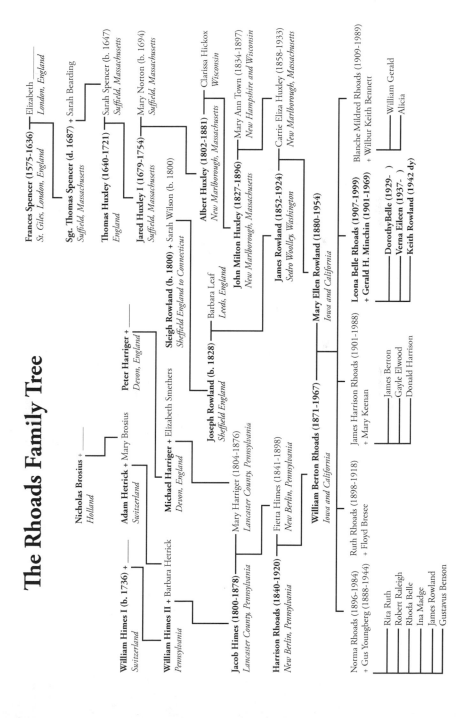

**Frances Spencer (1575-1636)**
*St. Giles, London, England*

Elizabeth
*London, England*

**Sgt. Thomas Spencer (d. 1687)** + Sarah Bearding
*Suffield, Massachusetts*

Sarah Spencer (b. 1647)
*Suffield, Massachusetts*

**Thomas Huxley (1640-1721)**
*England*

Mary Norton (b. 1694)
*Suffield, Massachusetts*

**Jared Huxley I (1679-1754)**
*Suffield, Massachusetts*

Clarissa Hickox
*Wisconsin*

**Albert Huxley (1802-1881)**
*New Marlborough, Massachusetts*

Mary Ann Town (1834-1897)
*New Hampshire and Wisconsin*

**John Milton Huxley (1827-1896)**
*New Marlborough, Massachusetts*

Carrie Eliza Huxley (1858-1933)
*New Marlborough, Massachusetts*

**James Rowland (1852-1924)**
*Sedro Woolley, Washington*

**Mary Ellen Rowland (1880-1954)**
*Iowa and California*

Blanche Mildred Rhoads (1909-1989)
+ Wilbur Keith Bennett

**Leona Belle Rhoads (1907-1999)**
**+ Gerald H. Minchin (1901-1969)**

William Gerald
Alicia

**Dorothybelle (1929- )**
**Verna Eileen (1937- )**
**Keith Rowland (1942 dy)**

**Nicholas Brosius** +
*Holland*

**Peter Harriger** +
*Devon, England*

**Adam Hetrick** + Mary Brosius
*Switzerland*

**Sleigh Rowland (b. 1800)** + Sarah Wilson (b. 1800)
*Sheffield England to Connecticut*

Barbara Leaf
*Leeds, England*

**Michael Harriger** + Elizabeth Smethers
*Devon, England*

**Joseph Rowland (b. 1828)**
*Sheffield England*

**William Himes I (b. 1736)** +
*Switzerland*

**William Himes II** + Barbara Hetrick
*Pennsylvania*

Mary Harriger (1804-1876)
*Lancaster County Pennsylvania*

**William Berton Rhoads (1871-1967)**
*Iowa and California*

James Berton
Gayle Elwood
Donald Harrison

James Harrison Rhoads (1901-1988)
+ Mary Keenan

**Jacob Himes (1800-1878)**
*Lancaster County Pennsylvania*

Fietta Himes (1841-1898)
*New Berlin, Pennsylvania*

**Harrison Rhoads (1840-1920)**
*New Berlin, Pennsylvania*

Ruth Rhoads (1898-1918)
+ Floyd Bresee

Rita Ruth
Robert Raleigh
Rhoda Belle
Ina Madge
James Rowland
Gustavus Benson

Norma Rhoads (1896-1984)
+ Gus Youngberg (1888-1944)